Deadly Impressions

PRAISE FOR ART JOHNSON AND *THE DEVIL'S VIOLIN*:

"Art Johnson is a master of at least two worlds....that of fiction writing and of music history. Just the best kind of book."

—*Author Tom Stern, M.D*

"If you like tightly written novels full of intrigue and mystery this book (*The Devil's Violin*) is for you!"

—*Patricia Statham, Top Reviewer*

"What a powerful and thrilling mystery!"

—*Zone Critic*

"This is a very clever and enjoyable story. It would be worth your while to read it. Very interesting and entertaining."

—*Jack Great Game, Top 500 Reviewer*

"Author Art Johnson has a clean, direct and to the point style of writing. A quick, entertaining Read, The Devil's Violin will keep you guessing."

—*Terrylynn, Top 500 Reviewer*

"The Devil's Violin is a haunting glimpse at not only mystery but the mysterious."

—*Ron Hogart,*

DEADLY IMPRESSIONS

ART JOHNSON

STORY MERCHANT BOOKS
LOS ANGELES
2015

THE STORY MERCHANT

Story Merchant Books
4009 S. Burnside Avenue #11B
Los Angeles, CA 90036

978-0-9963689-0-2

http://www.storymerchant.com/books.html

Cover art & interior design by IndieDesignz.com

For Flamenco Guitarist and art connoisseur, Robert Klein,
who passed away before this book was completed.

We miss you Bob.

Prologue

The sound of gravel crunching beneath the tires of Stephanie Fick's BMW 3.5 convertible pulled her out of a trance and back to reality. Last night had been a real one-off for the twenty-four year old. The pebbled lane soon gave way to smooth asphalt as she pulled into one of the private parking slots designated for her family.

"Beverly Hills Country Club — members only. Reserved for the Fick family."

The sign always made her smile. "The Fick family…" Hell, there was only her older brother Todd who lived in New York and had a seat on the stock exchange, and her billionaire grandfather, Ezekiel. Todd rarely came out to the west coast. She was just twelve when her parents died in a horrendous car crash on the interstate. At the time, Todd was turning seventeen and on his way to Harvard business school. He never looked back. With her parents gone, Stephanie was taken in by her grandfather.

The pretty, young and thoroughly spoiled blonde nervously lit a cigarette. What had prompted her best friend Doreen to push her into meeting the Club's new tennis coach from Italy yesterday? Doreen had known for weeks that she was engaged to Stanley Brunt, heir to the Brunt tire fortune. Okay, this guy from Rome, who is ranked in the top one hundred players in the world, was drop-dead gorgeous. And of course, it was only natural to book a lesson with him for this afternoon. God knows she could use all the help she could get with her game. But yesterday it would have been impossible to predict the outcome of that evening.

Mario Scarlatti was that picture-postcard-perfect man. Olive colored skin that was not greasy, about six feet tall with coal-black hair that seemed to be trained to drop a curl over one of his almond-colored eyes every time he laughed. And to top it off he had that very sexy unshaven one-day shadow that was so appealing on European men and so off-putting on Americans.

Go figure. It was about six o'clock in the evening when they met. Steph had no plans for the night. Her fiancée was in San Francisco with his mother. Mario invited her to the bar for a glass of wine. What could be more innocent? Who was she kidding? She was drooling over this guy the minute they met. She hadn't been with another man since she and Stanley made a commitment. Fuck, the word itself sounds like a jail sentence. What was she to do? A god-like figure, right out of the Greco/Roman pantheon stood before her with bedroom eyes and a statuesque body.

They grabbed a booth in the bar and after a bottle of pinot-noir and a few appetizers they moved closer for it was harder to hear each other as the room began to fill up. Their arms touched: electricity. From out of nowhere that uncontrollable impulse struck. They kissed. What a mistake this could have been if any of Stanley's friends or family had been in the bar. As it turned out, Freddy, the head bartender at the club who knows everyone and everything about everyone kindly looked the other way. Night fell.

God, what a night!

And here she was the day after, scheduled to face Mr. Incredible for a tennis lesson.

Change of plans. Her tires screeched in reverse tearing away from the family parking slot. She was out of here. And besides, here comes that creepy homeless person who is always hustling members for bogus charities. Why don't they keep these clowns off the premises?

Stephanie Fick, future heiress to the Fick industrial fortune, sped towards the exit. Distracted by her panic she failed to notice a late model sedan following her at a discreet distance as she pulled out of the parking lot.

She cut over Coldwater Canyon to pick up the Ventura freeway east and head home before dining with grandfather. She checked her rear-view mirror; a car seemed to be following her.

Paranoia, the disease of the rich and famous set in: that ever-present shadow of suspicion.

At the top of Coldwater she made a right hand turn onto Mulholland Drive just to test her intuition. The sedan was right behind her. She wished to hell she'd put the top up before she left the Country Club but it was too late to think about that now. She kept trying to convince herself that it was just her imagination running wild. Why would someone be following her? How would they know who she was? She was starting to hyperventilate and her palms were feeling sweaty on the steering wheel, slipping slightly as she took the snake like turns along Mulholland.

At this time of the day there were not many other cars traveling on this lonely stretch of the Drive. She gunned the motor making a quick U-turn, tires sounding like banshees wailing in her one hundred and eighty degree move out of desperation.

Too late.

The sedan was now perpendicular to the road blocking her way. She slammed on the brakes and looked behind her to peel out in reverse when a pair of muscular tattooed arms grabbed her around the neck and began choking her. A woman dove into the passenger seat and shut off the engine.

Stephanie tried to scream but it hurt too much, her throat was on fire. The man dragged her out of the car while the driver of the sedan watched. She kicked and flurried with her arms all the way but to no avail. Stephanie was strong and physically fit like her grandfather but she was no match for a gang on a mission to abduct her.

The driver of the sedan jumped out and opened the trunk. The woman applied duct tape across Stephanie's mouth. She could barely breathe. Her hands and feet were bound with plastic handcuffs. Adrenaline surged through her veins; she felt she might explode. She was shoved into the trunk of the sedan. The lid slammed shut with a loud bang.

Her mind was so jumbled she couldn't think. The car sped off bouncing her around in the cramped space. She never thought it would be like this.

Fade to black.

One

Private Investigator Arnold Blackburn had the same facial expression every time he was seated across from a drop-dead gorgeous woman: a look of focused indifference.

"Arney, you're the only one of my men friends who never put me down for being a lesbian."

The P.I. shifted on the bar stool. "…What's the problem? I'm with you one hundred percent. There's nothing more beautiful in the world than a woman's body."

His friend giggled. "You're a funny guy."

He stood up. "Yeah, just ask my ex-wife. Did you get that info I need?

The tiny blonde reached into her purse. "It wasn't easy this time—it's getting harder and harder to sneak it through."

"I appreciate it and I'll try not to take advantage too often."

She looked into his eyes after snapping her purse. "That's alright." She paused. "You know if I was into men, I'd take you right now on this table."

"Ooh….that'll give me something to think about tonight."

She watched him move as he left the bar. "God," she thought, "…if he was only a woman."

The recently installed private detective was adjusting to his new vocation after being kicked off the LAPD payroll for misconduct during a sting operation. It really wasn't his fault but a tendency to get a little bit carried away had always shadowed him.

Fortunately for Arney, L.A. Police Chief Fergus McCreary called him into his office the next day and moved through the paperwork *tout suite* for the now unemployed lawman to have a Private Detective's license in the County. There was method to the Police Chief's madness. He knew Arney to be a tried-and-true investigator that closed ninety per cent of his cases while with the department.

Chief Mac called Arney in as a consultant when the report of the potential kidnapping occurred. Ezekiel Fick's granddaughter had not been heard of since she left her tennis club yesterday afternoon. Fick and his billions had clout. He had the mayor of L.A. doing cartwheels to find out what had happened to her. They couldn't call in the FBI until it was official. People did walk-abouts all the time and there was, by law, a three day lag time before the Feds could be called to investigate a missing persons report.

Chief Mac wanted Arney to poke around on the other side of the fence to see if he could dig up any information regarding Stephanie Fick's disappearance. The police Chief knew that Blackburn would be a valuable piece on the chessboard as the situation developed.

After leaving the bar, the private-eye had just beeped his car door open when a hand the size of a catcher's mitt grabbed his left shoulder. He turned his head slowly to discover Bernard Needlebaum, right-hand man to Victor Gastaldi, one of L.A.'s most notorious loan-sharks and drug pushers. The big 'B' was not one of Arney's favorite people.

"…Been molesting any four year old boys recently Bern?"

Bernard squeezed tighter: Arney felt the pressure. "I haven't got time for you right now— Mr. Gastaldi wants to see you at your earliest inconvenience." He pulled a handgun out of his coat pocket.

Arney felt it pressed against his rib-cage. "It's your party pal."

The big 'B' led the way to the back seat of a mid-seventies Lincoln town car. The chauffeur pulled away with the two men locked in silence as they crept along Santa Monica heading east.

CHAPTER TWO

Born in east L.A. in 1981 from a father who was stabbed to death in prison with a prostitute for a mother, Victor Gastaldi was the real deal. He had gangster stamped onto his DNA.

When he was thirteen years old, he held up a liquor store with a toy gun yelling, "Hands up mother-sticker, this is a fuck up!" He immediately became the pride of his hood while at the same time launching a career which had been most successful over the past twenty years.

Victor was slim of build with a pair of eyes which could embrace you or sear through you like a laser pen-light. He was not personally prone to violence but maintained a staff to carry it out when necessary. The necessity appeared quite often in his mind. He employed over a dozen henchmen, each hand-picked.

Victor's headquarters located near MacArthur Park in East Los Angeles was an elegant Georgian mansion built in the nineteen twenties, showing its age like a fading film star hiding behind too much makeup. Fenced off from the surrounding streets, his fortress was also a 'no-cops' zone: a monthly cash payment delivered to the downtown precinct took care of that.

He wandered peacefully through the hallways of his two-story, ten room castle donning a wine-colored silk smoking jacket and a matching cravat. With a custom-rolled cigarette in an ivory holder in one hand, and his smartphone in the other, he was king of his domain.

Any minute now his special guest for the afternoon would be arriving.

The light in the room was dim. The floor-to-ceiling curtains in Victor Gastaldi's master bedroom were closed. Conchita Morales pulled the satin sheets and quilted comforter over her head, folded down the top portions with her hands and placed her arms at her side. She puffed up her cheeks and let the air out slowly. Rolling over to her left, the tiny Latina briefly checked her hair and makeup in a full length mirror near the bed. It was just a nervous reaction. It was so dark that she could barely make out her silhouette.

It had been a tough night. Victor had been in one of his moods.

The twenty-something prostitute had exhausted herself twice-over in an attempt to satisfy her lover but had failed. She had been working as a call girl for the Bigelow Brothers for over two years now and was in constant demand. Victor took a liking to her after their first encounter and cut a deal with the Brothers to have her as an exclusive.

However, tonight had not gone well.

In the early morning hours Victor stormed out leaving her alone. He didn't return. This was not a good sign. Either he was way pissed-off or some piece of business grabbed him. She prayed that it be the latter as she clamored out of bed to head for the shower.

After cruising Sunset past Vermont Avenue, Arney knew where they were headed when the driver took a right on Alvarado. Familiar territory. He himself lived in east Hollywood at the foot of the Silver Lake reservoir.

Arney didn't need any unscheduled meetings today. He was focused on his current case. The piece of paper that his contact at the hall of records had just slipped to him at the bar may be a lead. It was still in his pocket.

He weighed his options.

The doors to the Lincoln were not master-locked and at the next stop light he could just do a runner, but that would mean another encounter, possibly the next day. Better to get it over with. Besides, he was curious as to what Victor Gastaldi had on his mind.

He had only had one run-in with the notorious money-lender and drug czar while he was still on the force. Arney found Victor to be a shrewd manipulator who was able to stay calm under pressure and managed to land on his feet no matter how much evidence was stacked against him.

Besides, he'd always wanted to take a tour of the king's palace. Maybe his host would be serving a late lunch? One could always hope.

The entry gates of Gastaldi's mansion were on an electric beam. They opened slowly and the limo was greeted by two men who looked like world-wide-wrestling tag-team champs. Shaved heads, pecs full of steroids and matching goatees, the twins were also armed with identical H&K MP5 automatic weapons. Expressionless, they waved the car in with synchronized motion.

The initial view of the opulent 1920's structure caused Arney to think of "Citizen Kane" –Zanzibar! But the grounds were depressing. The front yard was full of weeds at least three feet tall: a fire hazard to say the least.

When the limo pulled up Victor was standing on the front porch flanked by two massive Doric marble columns chipped by time but still impressive. He was cuddling one of those small dogs Arney thought should be barbequed rather than kept as pets.

The gangster smiled maliciously as the big 'B' escorted Arney up the steps. Victor motioned to Bernie and his gun re-appeared. Victor patted Arney down with his free hand, the small dog whimpering all the while. When he was through he welcomed his guest. "Olá. Mid-day greetings Arney. Good to see you again."

Arney noticed how yellow Victor's teeth were. "Well Victor always nice to chum around with one of LA's finest financiers and providers of party-time treats."

Victor let out a howl of laughter causing him to drop the dog which scurried into the house. He placed his hand firmly on Arney's shoulder. "My god you're too much Blackburn, really full of it— follow me."

The mansion was cold inside and the walls looked moist. The aroma of mildew permeated the interior. The house gave Arney a creepy feeling as Victor guided him along scuffed and unvarnished wood floors to a room at the end of the hallway.

Conchita Morales heard footsteps and voices downstairs and assumed that Victor was having a meeting. She crept down the carpeted stairs to go to the kitchen for a bite to eat.

Arney sat on a leather chair in what must have been the original library. Glancing around the room he saw the figure of Conchita slip by the doorway. He knew she was one of the Bigelow Brothers working girls. So Victor and the Bigelow's were pals—interesting.

Arney was offered a cigar but declined. "So, what brings me to your casa this bright, Thursday afternoon Victor?"

Gastaldi shot a quick glance towards Bernard and he and the chauffeur left the room. Victor sniffed his cigar before lighting it. He looked up at Arney. "Let's see…the last time we saw each other you were a cop—and now you're not. My sources tell me that since leaving the department you've become a private detective."

"That's been my career of choice for the past few weeks, is there a problem?"

Victor pounded his cigar on the rim of the ash tray trying to dump an ash which had not formed yet. "Oh no… nothing like that, I just thought that we might do a little business."

Arney was curious. "Well Victor, it's your call, I'm listening."

Victor relaxed his shoulders and sat back in his chair. "You ever heard of Danny Ballantyne?"

The private eye thought for a second. "Nope, name doesn't ring a bell, what gives?"

Victor pointed his cigar towards the ash tray. This time there was an ash. "He's a big shot out of Chicago, newly arrived on our pleasant coastline. I'd like you to keep an eye on him for me. Rumor has it that he'd like to walk in my shoes. Of course, this is not possible. My shoes are Ferragamos from Italy, very expensive and only my feet fit comfortably in them, if you get my drift."

Arney felt a slight discomfort. "Haven't you got enough manpower to handle the situation yourself?"

"Oh I have some of the best fire power in the business. It's just that this situation requires a little finesse and my boys can't even spell the word." Victor paused. "...Besides, Mr. Ballantyne might have a bit of information that you would find very helpful right now." Victor paused to engage eye contact with his guest. "I believe that you are unofficially part of the team investigating the possibility of a young woman from Pasadena who has disappeared and may have been kidnapped?

Arney started to respond, Victor waved him off. "I have my informants just like any other business man. It always pays to stay in touch with current events."

The private detective was in such a state of shock that he lit his cigar. He was a non-smoker.

Since the disappearance of Pasadena billionaire Ezekiel Fick's granddaughter, the police had come up with very little. It had been two days since she was last heard from.

Victor was hinting that it might be a kidnapping and that out-of-town forces were involved.

Arney dropped his cigar into the ashtray seconds after he lit it. "So, you think this guy Ballantyne may have something to do with her disappearance?"

Victor smiled that confident smile any salesman has at his disposal when he knows the hook has been set in the gills. "Well, my informants are pretty reliable. Let's just say that we can kill two birds with one stone by scratching each other's back...what say amigo?"

The thought of even seeing Victor's bareback made Arney's skin crawl. "Where is Ballantyne?"

Arney realized how confident Victor was of his co-operation as he slid a pre-prepared manila envelope across the desk. "Everything you need to know is in here including my private cell number and the hotel on Sunset where he is currently installed. I'll be expecting to hear from you daily with a report."

"And what if I don't care to play your little game?"

Victor smiled exposing his yellowed teeth. "Well amigo, you want Fick's granddaughter returned safely and I'm prepared to do what I can in the way of poking around on my own to assist you. All I ask is that you keep an eye on an individual which could be a problem to us both. It doesn't sound that unreasonable to me."

Arney paused. "Well, one thing for sure is that if her disappearance is due to the fact that she was abducted the Feds will be here any minute now to take charge. They'll be at the top of the pecking order and I will probably be considered excess baggage."

Victor smiled. "Maybe— maybe not. If you can nail this Danny dude before they arrive the feather is in your cap."

Arney gathered up the envelope staring at Victor's snide smile. "Just what kind of fee can I expect for doing this little deed for the Gastaldi empire?"

Victor laughed. "Look inside bro. I think the enclosed check will cover your expenses and then some."

Arney nodded. "I'll keep you posted."

He passed through the iron gates of the mansion bidding farewell to the WWW tag-team champions and grabbed a cab on the east side of MacArthur Park.

Three

The heart of Long Beach, California hadn't changed much in the past fifty years. There were still mom-and-pop shops and a lazy harbor where locals moored their boats.

Zoltin Slim paged through the selections on the table juke box in his favorite 50's style diner on Cherry Avenue. He was chewing on his ever-present toothpick, a habit he'd picked up at the age of ten and continued to this day forty years later. His muscular tattooed arms were still scratched up from his latest assignment. That little rich bitch put up a good fight. He admired that in a woman. Now that she was tucked away in a safe house a few blocks from the diner he could relax and enjoy a few moments of Miles Davis on the jukebox.

Zoltin Slim was one of the most respected evil energies on the scene. An experienced hit-man and muscle for hire, his reputation circulated through dark corridors in mythic proportions. No one ever fucked with Mr. Slim.

Enjoying his 'all-you-can-drink' coffee in the traditional brown-with-age porcelain cup he was about to drop a quarter in the slot to hear Miles play "It never entered my mind" from 1952 when his cell phone went off.

Zoltin hated the damn thing. He despised everything that had been invented past the year 1963. Though his current employer requested that he have a smart-phone, Zoltin refused, accepting only the simplest of disposable cell-phones. This bad man could call his own shots. He was top in his field.

Penny, the waitress whom had been serving customers at the diner for at least three decades, brought Zoltin a chocolate shake.

"Hey honey, you have one more of these and you'll be sweet enough to eat." He smiled as she walked away, wanting to stab her in the back repeatedly and watch the blood ooze out.

He was having happy thoughts as his ears were caressed by the soft strains of the muted trumpet before cruising out the door, heading for his Harley Davidson— a KH model from the 1950's.

Four

During his cab ride back to West L.A., Arney read the print-out he received in the bar. Over the years, he had gathered a handful of good informants whose talents had paid off while he was on the force. Fortunately, since his departure from the LAPD, most of them were still there for him.

One street wise person was Chad Sillietoe. A professional hustler and panhandler, it was rumored that his annual income exceeded that of many suits holding down nine to fivers.

Arney knew that Chad worked the high-end districts. He contacted him to see if he might have been in Beverly Hills the afternoon of Stephanie Fick's disappearance. It paid off. Chad was hustling the members of the Beverly Hills Tennis Club in the parking lot, fictiticusly collecting money for the Jerry Lewis telethon due to be on the air that weekend.

Chad had approached the Fick heiress with a big smile only to be waved off as she was leaving the club. That was just after four o'clock in the afternoon. His eyes followed her car as it left and he noticed a dark sedan immediately in pursuit. For no other reason than the mere coincidence of the fact that the numbers on the license plate were the same as Chad's birthdate,"11-13-65" he had remembered them. Also helpful was the huge Hertz rent-a-car sticker on the rear bumper.

Arney's friend at the DMV had run the numbers through the nationwide Hertz computer and had found a match. "11-13-65" was leased three days ago by Daniel Ballantyne of 3158 Lake Shore Drive, Chicago. The DMV also coughed up his CV of criminal activities over the past two decades. Impressive.

Leaving the cab in West Hollywood, Arney peeled the parking ticket off of his windshield and sat in the front seat. He dumped the contents of the envelope Victor gave him onto the passenger side.

There were three photos of Danny Ballantyne. Arney guessed him to be in his mid-forties, dressed in a white suit with a blue button-down shirt and a wildly colorful, floral print tie. He looked like a Hollywood film producer trying to be noticed without trying to be noticed.

There was a business card in Victor's name with all of the printed numbers scratched off and a penciled number scrawled on the back. Also a check made out to cash for far too much money and a set of keys. He tore up the check and examined the keys. Blank. The last item in the envelope was the number of a suite at the Hilton on Sunset, just west of La Cienega where Ballantyne was supposedly staying.

Arney tucked the hotel room number into his coat pocket and put the other items back into the envelope placing it under the passenger seat. He stared down at his steering wheel for a few seconds, started the car and headed home.

He'd check out the Hilton tonight to see if Mr. Ballantyne was receiving guests.

CHAPTER FIVE

While P.I. Blackburn was being entertained by Victor Gastaldi, Ezekiel Fick was seated on the garden terrace of his opulent Pasadena residence.

He was glancing through the Wall Street Journal without paying any attention while sipping tea and nibbling on fresh scones prepared by his pastry chef. His eyes darted constantly towards his cell phone lying on the table, willing it to ring.

Grandfather Fick's physical appearance defied his eighty years. He looked more like a man in his mid-sixties. He was obsessed about staying young as long as possible. He played three rounds of golf a week and worked out daily in his own private gym on the premises. Each morning when he first rose out of bed he was down on the floor doing fifty pushups before taking a pee.

The multi-billionaire set his tea cup down momentarily engaged by the overlapping melodies of bird-songs ringing throughout the foliage of his garden.

His reverie was broken by the beep of his cell phone. Only six persons on the face of the planet had this number including the President of the United States. He looked down at the caller ID—it was Stephanie. He rushed to pick up the phone and knocked the tea cup onto the patio smashing it to smithereens. He punched the talk button: 'Steph—is that you... are you OK?" Silence. He spoke again, more silence.

He was about to hang up when a whispered voice began. "Go to Griffith Park tonight at eight o'clock, alone, first bench on the left after entering Ferndell." Before he could reply the phone went dead. He punched re-dial and got Stephanie's voice mail. The sound of her voice made him cry.

Making a quick recovery, he speed-dialed the mayor with the latest information, who in turn notified Chief McCreary in a panic. The head of Los Angeles' finest closed his office door and called P.I. Blackburn at his home.

Arney was in the shower when he heard his phone. Wrapped in a towel and dripping wet, he listened to the message. It was more than likely going to be a very long night; time to call in the cavalry.

He couldn't be two places at once.

CHAPTER SIX

LAPD Sergeant Gary Bub was undoubtedly the poster-boy for the link between the police force and donuts. He consumed at least a dozen a day.

His dedication to this strict diet was more than demonstrated on one occasion when he and his partner were in hot pursuit of a stolen car. Bub happened to spot a Winchell's donut shop a block away. He accelerated past the stolen vehicle, pulled into the parking lot, jumped out, went inside, grabbed a box of variety assortment and dove back into his squad car without missing a beat. They nabbed the culprit five blocks away and Bub's rookie partner spread the story about his sugar crazed Sergeant as soon as they got back to the precinct.

Chief McCreary got wind of the incident and rather than reprimanding the twenty-year veteran, sent the sweet-toothed policeman two dozen glazed-chocolate jumbos from the original Dunkin' Donuts on Centinela near LAX. Gary Bub, in spite of his weakness for sugary, cake-like treats, was one of L.A.'s finest and had taken bullets twice in the line of duty, saving several lives in the past two decades.

He was just opening the front door of his Highland Avenue apartment when his cell-phone went off. He smiled at the caller-ID; it was Arnold Blackburn, one of the few cops, now an ex-cop that Bub continued to respect: in Bub's mind they were brothers.

"Yo, Philip Marlowe, how's the private-dick business; more dick than business....or?"

"Fuck you fat man, I need a favor and this is serious."

The cop stood in the doorway of his apartment with a bag of groceries between his legs and listened to his friend intently. After finishing the call, Bub prepared for his stake-out that night on the Sunset Strip.

Seven

Zoltin Slim stopped his Harley down an alleyway off Eighth Avenue and Long Beach Boulevard. He opened up a small garage door and rolled the bike inside. He locked the door, looked both ways down the alley, took out a fresh toothpick and strolled lazily heading east towards Clinton Street four blocks away. Mid-way down the block he crossed the lawn of a small craft-style house, went through the front door, down the hallway, through the kitchen, walked out the back door, locked it and crossed over the rear fence to enter the side door of a small garage belonging to another residence, on the adjacent street.

The structure had all its windows blackened out and stuffed with sound-proofing material. It was not visible from the street and the house it belonged to was empty.

Inside, the garage was divided into two rooms. Zoltin paused in the first to observe the activities being displayed on four monitors his partner had set up, fed by a series of surveillance cameras positioned around the property which were being fed into a laptop computer.

There was a separate monitor which was focused on the activities going on in the next room. Zoltin removed a second key from his pocket and pushed it into the industrial quality deadbolt, turning the key four times before the door would open. "Hey Dee, what's goin' on?"

Dee Dee Jameson was seated on a chair with an automatic handgun across her lap. Zoltin entered the sound-proof chamber.

"Wha's up cousin?" Dee-Dee stood and stretched her muscular arms offering a friendly punch to Zoltin's left bicep.

Zoltin had never quite understood gay persons. A man was a man and a woman was a woman and the opposites fit together and that's the end of it.

Dee-Dee Jameson was thirty-five years old and had been married in her twenties and divorced by her husband two years ago. She knew something wasn't right while still married when the large breasted blonde waitress who was serving the couple dinner at a local restaurant followed Dee into the ladies room and stood behind her while facing the bathroom mirror. She smiled as she began to fondle Dee's petite breasts while nibbling on her neck. At first Dee tightened up but within seconds, as she watched the action in the mirror, she realized that this was what she had been missing.

At the age of thirty-two, when her final divorce was official, Dee came out of the closet and made up rapidly for lost time. Over the years of sexual experimentation she gravitated towards the male role and quickly found herself building muscle at the neighborhood gym, acquiring a few meaningful tattoos and a collection of body piercing statements.

Her face was still very pretty although she no longer wore makeup. She was five-foot six, long-wasted, virtually flat-chested and carried herself with a manly swagger. Never the less, she was still fighting off men who were more than attracted to a butch dyke with the face of an angel.

Zoltin and Dee now stood next to a bed which nearly took up all the space of room number two. Stephanie Fick's hands were tied to the bed posts, while her feet were left unbound. Mr. Slim took out a fresh toothpick. "How's she doin' today?"

Dee stared down somewhat affectionately, eyeing her clothed body from tip to toe.

"Oh, she's been a good girl and taken her medicine just like auntie says."

Stephanie's eyes were covered with a sleeping mask. She could hear but not see her captors. From sheer adrenaline, Stephanie's nipples had grown hard and were protruding through her blouse.

Zoltin sensed Dee's excitement. "Hands off mister. This package must be kept unused…get my drift? That order comes from the one above us all."

Dee snickered. "You mean God gives a shit if I cop a little feel from miss white-toast?"

Zoltin didn't look at Dee as he said, "God ain't nothin' compared to the hombre who hired me. I have to answer to him and you answer to me." The tattooed heavy then turned his gaze in Dee's direction and fixed his cold steel eyes on hers. "I even catch you kissing her on the cheek and you'll be outta here with no one to turn to and nowhere to hide—believe me, I ain't fuckin' around."

As tempting as the twenty-four year old was, Dee knew Zoltin's reputation before they began to work together. She answered him with a smile.

"You got it Z…."

Eight

Shadows—nothing but shadows.

Not the same as pure darkness.

There is movement of some kind but I can't feel my body.

There is a constant wind. Do you hear it? Can you feel it?

I think I am moving but I'm not...can't seem to focus on where I am or why I'm here?

I must be dreaming but I never wake up. Someone pinches me every so often and then the shadows grow darker.

I begin to hear strange music...nothing like I've ever heard before; muffled voices as if some choir were rehearsing in another room.

Death is like this, yes? I believe so. It is peaceful, yet I'm afraid.

I'm afraid of not dying completely.

Never knowing true death— only an imitation.

Why am I here? Where am I?

Stephanie had moments where she remembered the last day she saw the sun. It was so long ago. Her hallucinations were constant.

One moment she would be at the beach where it was snowing and icy cold. Then she would find herself walking on a dirt path cutting through a deep forest with a hooded man alongside her speaking very low. She would bend toward him to hear what he was saying but when she could a voice inside her told her that it was an ancient language spoken before Christ was born.

And oh yes…she had seen the Christ many times when he brought her bread to eat, and also the Virgin Mary when she gave her a hug.

Then there were the times when the dream gave way for a brief moment and Stephanie could feel that she was in serious trouble. In these lucid moments she wanted to scream but nothing came out. After all, it was just a game…right?

Shadows—nothing but shadows.

CHAPTER NINE

Nine

Following Chief Mac's orders, Arney arrived at Griffith Park by seven forty-five. He strolled lazily in the direction of Ferndell with a copy of the L.A. Times tucked under his arm.

The path to the left where the benches were located wound its way along a rivulet of water that ran the length of the grove for about a quarter of a mile. He decided to walk the whole left-side embankment and then arrive in time to catch the activity, if any, at bench number one.

As he descended the path the elder Fick sat nervously with a briefcase while looking left and right in a constant motion. Having seen a photo of the tycoon, but never having met him Arney realized that the distressed grandfather might think he was the contact. He picked up his pace and moved rapidly. Once he exited the entrance he went across the street and plopped down on the vast lawn to read his paper. He had a perfect view of the bench.

For a moment he lost himself. He hadn't been back to Griffith Park since he and his father came here in the late-eighties to play ball or just hike around. His father had been a top journalist for the L.A. Times. He kept late hours but always had time for his son whom he adored.

One night a squad car showed up at the family residence around two o'clock in the morning. Arney could hear his mother crying all the way from his bedroom in the back of the house. The police had shown up to deliver the bad news. Witnesses had found the forty-nine year old newspaper-man shot in the head, execution style seated behind the steering wheel of his car in the parking lot across the street from the Times building. Arney knew his father was working on a special assignment for the Times that involved L.A. racketeers. The nine year old decided then and there to become a cop.

Eight o'clock came and went as the two men waited. The old man was fidgety. His left leg was bouncing up and down with nervous energy and his head was in constant motion. At precisely a quarter past eight, the old man's cell phone went off. Arney tried to listen but Fick's voice was inaudible.

After the call the billionaire looked behind the bench and retrieved a small package. He took the palm-sized object and scurried off. Arney waited for two minutes and then casually walked back to his car.

He could now call Chief Mac and tell him what took place: a no-show with a pre-planted package. Stephanie Fick's disappearance could now be officially tagged as a kidnapping.

It was time to call Gary Bub and see how things were going at the Sunset Hilton. Hopefully, Danny Ballantyne was still hanging around.

CHAPTER TEN

The lounge bar at the Hilton on Sunset was sparsely dotted with persons having a drink while nibbling on bar-mix nuts and chips.

LAPD Sergeant Gary Bub settled himself into a comfortable arm chair next to a small bistro table with a view of the lobby and entrance to the hotel. A tall, slender bald-headed waiter plopped down a napkin. "Have you got any donuts?"

The server shifted on his feet with a perturbed expression. "Tell me sir, do you think this is a hotel or a Winchel's?"

Bub opened his coat just wide enough to expose his belt-mounted LAPD badge and weapon. "Oh, I just thought you might keep a few around for the kids…you know what I mean?"

Attitude refreshed, the waiter said he'd see what he could do. Gary Bub nodded and called the hotel to see if Mr. Ballantyne was still a guest. From his table in the lounge he had a full view of the front desk. He watched the receptionist as she answered his call and confirmed the fact that Mr. Ballantyne was still registered but was not in the hotel at the moment.

Gary thanked her and hung up. Now it was just about the waiting. Waiting was a cop's meditation: an ingrained discipline—the yoga of patience.

The waiter returned with a plate full of the tasty treats ten minutes later. Bub was on his third morsel when he spied a man whom he thought to be Ballantyne walking into the hotel with what might be one of the Bigelow Brother's call girls on his arm. He went straight to the front desk with his babe in tow and said something to the receptionist. Her voice carried. Gary Bub could just hear her say, "No Mr. Ballantyne, nothing at the moment."

Bub's cell phone vibrated. "Hey Gary, Arney. Anything going on?"

"Ballantyne just arrived with some of the high-priced-spread heading off to paradise on the fourteenth floor. Want me to go take a peek?"

"I'm there in two minutes, just parking the car. Where are you?"

Bub took a bite. "I'm downing my third donut at the lobby bar. I'll wait for you... copy?"

"I'm just around the corner."

Less than two minutes later Arney entered the lobby but Bub was nowhere to be seen.

Time for a pee, Arney thought so he took a bar stool and waited. Five minutes went by, then ten. Something wasn't right. He called Bub's cell but it went straight to voice-mail.

Arney entered the hotel men's room. Nothing. He then went to reception and asked the girl at the desk if she had seen his friend? He struck out again. He went back to the bar and asked for the waiter that had served Bub. When the server arrived he could be of no help. A feeling of panic struck like lightning. His began to scour around the lobby looking for a clue.

He heard a woman scream. Arney ran in the direction of the commotion. People were starting to gather around. He feared the worse.

A woman ran out of the ladies room in a panic. Arney dashed in to find Bub face down on the floor, shot from behind. Blood was oozing everywhere. He felt his pulse—still there.

The sound of sirens shrieked down Sunset. Three LAFD paramedics rushed in. After taking Bub's vitals one of them gave Arney the high sign. "We'll get him out of here and over to Cedars. It's serious but he'll make it."

Arney dashed for the elevator, punched fourteen, and waited for what seemed an eternity for the doors to open. Suite 1406 was arrowed to the left. With his Colt 9m drawn he cautiously made his way down the hall. He stood at the entrance and listened. He could hear noises from other rooms but not from 1406.

He knocked three times and waited.

He banged his fist twice more, still no response.

A cleaning woman came down the hall pushing her cart.

He ordered her over flashing his old police badge.

She keyed the door and stepped back as if this was routine.

Arney bolted in, weapon raised and ready. The suite was empty: no luggage, no ruffled bed clothes and no used water glasses. It looked as if the room hadn't been unoccupied all day. He checked both rooms and the bathroom then went back to find the cleaning lady.

"Where's the man who was staying in this suite?"

"There hasn't been anyone in this room since yesterday."

Arney looked confused. "You mean there's been no one named Ballantyne in this room?"

She smiled, "Oh him, he moved to the 12th floor, number 1208. He's a real nice man out of Chicago I believe and a big tipper..."

Arney headed for the stairwell. He ran down to the twelfth floor landing where he was met by four of L.A.'s finest. Although he told them who he was and what he was doing they still removed his hand gun, cuffed him and took him downstairs. He came out of the elevator in a rage face to face with Chief McCreary. Arney was yelling about Ballantyne but no one was listening.

"Jesus Christ Arney, what in the hell is going on?" Mac ordered the cuffs removed and Arney's weapon returned then the Chief escorted him to an empty office behind the reception desk. The aging lawman slammed the door and rubbed his eyes in exasperation before digging in. "What in the hell are you yelling about and what were you and Bub up to anyway? All I asked you to do was a bit of surveillance on Fick and now I've got a cop at Cedars in critical condition!" Fergus took a break to breathe; his face was red.

Arney jumped in. "He's getting away— the guy who shot Bub is in 1208. Send a crew up there immediately!" Arney was screaming at his former boss.

McCreary ripped his walkie-talkie off of its Velcro patch and gave the order to hold the occupants of 1208. "What happened with Fick tonight? He called me when he arrived home and told me that no one showed up, is that true?"

Arney collected himself. "He's lying. It was a no-show but someone called him on his cell and guided him to a small package behind the bench. Fick grabbed it and ran. I waited around for a couple of minutes then I came here to meet up with Bub."

Just then there was a knock at the door. A female officer stepped through. "…Sent a detail up to 1208, Chief. No one there; looks like they did a runner. Forensics is dusting for prints and giving the room a once-over but that's all we've got so far." The woman gave Arney a dirty look as she left.

McCreary rubbed his eyes again. "Why in the hell was Bub here in the first place? Who were you two tailing and why? I think it's time we start right from the beginning. I know you Blackburn. You're holding something back."

Arney straightened up in his chair and began to recount his meeting with Victor Gastaldi.

Chief Mac listened intently.

Eleven

The hand-carved mahogany walls of the mansion's library seemed to close in around Ezekiel Fick as he sat at his desk and nervously un-wrapped the scotch-taped box. He had a decanter of seventy-year old malt whisky by his side with a fine crystal tumbler half-empty near his right hand.

He held the box up to the light. It looked like a Tiffany's ring box. Removing the top he found a flash drive cushioned on a bed of cotton—no note of any kind. He stared at it for a long time.

"What could this be?" He asked himself. "Where in the hell is my Stephanie?" The powerful industrialist looked like a weakened cripple as he bent over his computer and slid the drive into the slot. He powered up and punched a few keys. The drive was now installed. He poured another dram of whisky downing the liquor in one gulp and hit the enter button.

It was a video. The first scene was a shot fixed on a wide exposure of land. A mountainous region full of dense forests and dapples of snow as if winter was receding and spring were due. Fick watched intensely but his darting eyes did not recognize the area. Very slowly, the camera panned to the extreme left, exposing more forests and sloping hill-sides.

Then the camera panned back toward the original fixed shot and moved to the right exposing more dense forests.

Ezekiel was trying desperately to understand what all of this had to do with Stephanie—where was she?—is she in some cabin in a remote region? When the camera finally came to a halt, it had fixed its lens upon a small village in the distance. Slowly, the shot zoomed in on a tower in the midst of other dwellings.

His memory was coming to life. This video was not filmed in America. Those mountains and the ancient church steeple could only be one place—the place where he was raised, in an isolated region of Switzerland. He froze. Dark thoughts overcame him.

The screen went to black and then in a few seconds a new scene appeared: a small room. He gasped when he saw Stephanie, masked and tied to a bed. She was making small groaning noises and appeared to be drugged.

"…Oh my God!" The panic shot him back in his chair. The scene lasted a little over a minute. Within a few seconds three words appeared—

"*Do you remember?*"

Then the program shut down. The room took on a menacing calm.

The wealthy industrialist couldn't move—his face froze— jaw clenched—his fists tightened until his knuckles turned blue.

He remembered.

For the first time in over six decades he was afraid; fearful of the past and what bearing it may have on the present.

The mayor of Los Angeles had been staying in contact with the anxious billionaire. Rich people just get special attention and that's all there is to it. When you are someone who consults with the President of the United States, you automatically have privileges.

Just as the video concluded, the city's leader called to tell him that law enforcement now had evidence that Stephanie had been abducted.

A resident along Mulholland Drive was out walking his dog and witnessed a young woman being dragged out of her BMW by two men and a woman who then stuffed the screaming victim into the trunk of a sedan and sped away. The patrol officer who arrived to take the man's report ran the license plate of the abandoned BMW and it was registered to Ms. Fick.

The mayor was breathing heavily. "I'm sorry to have to be the one to tell you about this but I thought you'd like to know that two of the best FBI Agents in Southern California had been assigned to the case." The mayor paused to get a reaction but the billionaire said nothing. "They'll be here any minute."

Fick thanked the mayor, hung up the phone and poured himself another big scotch. He re-ran the video and kept drinking. About an hour later his butler came into the library with a dinner tray and quietly exited. The old man ate tepidly for a few minutes. *Do you remember?* The phrase kept repeating over and over in his head.

How could he forget? He was so young, so scared, so determined. He offered himself another dram of whisky and settled back in his chair, closing his eyes. The images of the video raced through Ezekiel's mind. The forest, the village, Stephanie tied down to a bed. The old man's imagination was filled with the fear of what she may be going through this very moment in her captivity.

Memory took over and it seemed as if a movie were running on the back of his eyelids.

The year was 1944. Ezekiel Fick was twelve years old. Years earlier, when Hitler invaded Poland, his father moved the family from Germany to Switzerland in an attempt to live out the war in peace. However, Ezekiel's uncle Roderich had embraced Hitler's master plan. He was an extremely gifted architect whose talent did not go unnoticed by the Fuehrer.

One portion of Hitler's egomaniacal master plan was to have a magnificent art museum designed in the Greco-Roman style to be built in Linz, Austria to house the mass of European works of art which the Nazis began to confiscate in 1939. Over one hundred thousand pieces including paintings, books, silver, religious objects, furniture and sculpture were to be housed in the Fuehrer museum which was never to be. Hitler chose Roderich Fick to manifest this vision into reality.

Sitting in the stilled darkness of his library Ezekiel Fick recalled the weekend during the war when his famous uncle traveled from Berlin to visit the family.

Roderich Fick was a gregarious man of huge proportions. Young Ezekiel idolized him believing he could build a house with his bare hands. The boy had seldom heard his father laugh except in the company of his prestigious brother.

Ezekiel remembered listening from his bed to the night-long conversation his father and uncle had until he fell asleep. Actually, he couldn't make out one word of their exchange but their murmurs reached intense levels and then quieted down to whispers in the same way the Beethoven symphonies had sounded over the family radio each night.

One morning Uncle Roderich invited Ezekiel to take a walk in the forest. Once they were out of sight they sat in a small clearing. The man reached into his coat pocket and took out a small manila envelope sealed with tape. He smiled down affectionately at his nephew.

"My boy, a new world is dawning." Roderich looked around as if he were expecting an intruder. "Germany under the divine guidance of the Fuehrer will soon rule the entire globe. The German people will control the destiny of the future. Adolf Hitler has seen through his unique vision the coming of a super-race capable of accomplishing the deeds of gods." Roderich paused to wipe his brow with his handkerchief. "In this envelope is the key to your future. What I am about to tell you is in the strictest of confidence."

The young Ezekiel thought he was looking at a giant.

"Your father has a rare disease and will not live much longer. This package contains an address and a key. Do not open it until your father passes away. Then, and only then, are you to follow the instructions. From that point on you will be on your own with the knowledge of what to do next."

Ezekiel began to cry as his uncle spoke but he soon wiped his tears away in a gesture of strength. "What am I to do until that day, uncle? How can I go home and carry on as usual with what you have just told me?"

Roderich tightened his grip on the young boy's shoulders and smiled down at him. "You will survive and conquer your fears, trust me."

The pair walked back to the chalet in silence, the only sound the crackle of dry leaves beneath their feet on the forest floor.

CHAPTER TWELVE

A light drizzle began as Arney parked his car at Cedars Sinai. He had debated all morning as to whether or not to show up. He wanted to know how his friend was doing but he was no longer a cop. L.A.'s finest would be there along with Bub's ex-wife Carolyn and the three boys. He just couldn't get past the guilt issue.

Chief Mac spotted him and gave him a nod. He felt better but still didn't feel like he belonged. He avoided eye contact with everyone around him. The doctors had issued a general bulletin for police officials: Bub would live, but may not gain complete control over his right arm. The bullet had entered his back and exited out his left shoulder tearing through some tendons and nerves along the path.

Arney decided to leave. As he walked out a young boy came up and asked him if he were Mr. Blackburn. Arney nodded and the kid handed him an envelope then ran off. Inside was a sheet of paper with four words and a cell-phone number. "It was a mistake 323-650-9874."

He sat in his car staring at the message. He dialed the number. It went directly to a standard answering message, "The caller is not available at this time…"

Arney was beginning to believe his anonymous confessor. "It was a mistake…"

The light mist was turning into a mild rain that blurred the front window of the car and could be heard falling on the roof. After his visit to Griffith Park last night Arney knew that it was officially a kidnapping and that the Feds would be on the scene any minute now. His time to search for the victim would be limited. Arney pulled out the photos of Danny Ballantyne that Victor had given him earlier that day.

It hit him like a piano dropped out of a tenth floor window—Bub and Ballantyne viewed from a distance could be the same person: Same height, same build and weight. Whoever shot Gary Bub might have just mistaken him for the Chicago gangster.

Tonight he would pay Victor Gastaldi a surprise visit. That son of a bitch knows more than he's copping to. Arney smiled as he anticipated getting past Huey and Dewey at the front gate. He was in the mood for some fun.

As he entered his house the phone was ringing. It was Chief Mac. "I wanted to talk with you before you left the hospital today, why'd you disappear?"

Arney took a deep breath. "Just didn't feel right."

"It wasn't your fault son, it's just the roll of the dice. Christ, I may as well blame myself for Bub's injuries. I got you into this mess with the Fick family. There never has been or will there ever be a reason for anything that happens to people like us who choose the way we travel down the road. You win a few, you lose a few—you live, you die: that's all there is to it, it doesn't get any deeper than that."

Arney was not in a philosophical mood. "What do you want?"

McCreary continued without skipping a beat. "We got a report today from an eyewitness along Mulholland Drive who watched Stephanie Fick being abducted the day she disappeared."

Arney drew a breath. "Then it's official. The Feds will be on the scene?"

"Yeah, they'll be here shortly to take charge." But Chief Mac had more on his mind. "I spoke with Fick this morning before coming to the hospital. He swore to me that there was no package behind the bench in the park and that whoever told me that was a goddamn liar."

Arney cut in. "Fick's full of shit. He grabbed the package and ran off like a scared puppy. Hell, the more I think about it, the more I'm inclined to think that the son of a bitch staged the kidnapping himself for some reason or reasons unknown and now it's all backfiring on him."

The Chief paused to think then responded. "Why would he do that? He's on the phone half the day with the mayor. I've got a feeling that by the time the Feds get organized we're going to find the victim raped with her throat cut stretched out in some bowery side-street or stuffed in a dumpster in the valley. We've got to stay on this as long as we have the jurisdiction to do so. Pull yourself together Blackburn, I need you on this one."

Arney walked around the Silver Lake reservoir a few times, came back home, took a short nap and waited for darkness to fall. Around 9:30 he checked his hand gun. Before leaving he left a message with a friend at the phone company to see if they could trace the cell phone number that was written on the note.

Snacking on a sandwich and a cup of coffee while staring at the street lamp's rippled reflections on the lake, he wished he had a row boat. This kidnapping was a confusing mess.

If Victor Gastaldi is right, why would someone hire a Chicago bad guy to do the deed when there are plenty of qualified hoodlums on every street corner in L.A.?

Was the perpetrator pulling the strings and laying out the cash for this kidnapping local, national or international? What was in the package that Fick walked off with last night? Is Stephanie Fick already dead? Is she being held somewhere in L.A. County or out of state? Maybe, after a visit to Gastaldi's mansion with his Colt in the crime-boss's face Arney might finally have some answers.

Downtown L.A. was fogged in.

Arney approached Gastaldi's property dressed in black with matching Nike climbing slippers. He walked around until he found a sagging spot in the surrounding wall. He vaulted over in one clean motion and paused to listen.

It was nearly eleven o'clock and the only lights came from the second floor. Arney had a clear view of the front gate. The two dumbbell brothers must be off for the night—he was sorry to postpone the laughs.

Moving cautiously through the weeds towards the house he was on the lookout for any signs of a guard dog. So far, so good. Victor's four vintage cars were parked near the garage but there was another vehicle that had low-rider written all over it. Victor was probably upstairs cooking a drug deal. Arney moved along the left hand side of the house heading for the rear entrance when a pistol's cold-steel muzzle pressed hard against his neck.

A voice from behind; it was the big 'B'. "Goin' somewhere Blackburn?"

Arney tried to keep it light. "…Just inspecting the property Bern. You know the fire department would raise hell with all these dry weeds around the building, but between you and me, I won't tell if you won't."

Bernie Needlebaum removed Arney's piece. "Well, we should probably inform the owner of this dilemma who fortunately for both of us is home at the moment. Let's pay him a visit shall we?" Arney anticipated the blow just before he felt it then all went black.

When he awoke, the second-story office was spinning slightly but Victor Gastaldi's eyes were burning into his. "Well, well detective Blackburn, we meet up twice in one week. What do I owe the honor of your presence on this balmy evening?"

The stunned detective shook his head. "No guessing games, Victor. You know why I'm here. Why in the hell did you send someone to off Ballantyne that couldn't tell the difference between Bub and the bad guy?"

Victor lit a cigarette and pulled a chair up opposite Arne. "Whoa! You're moving way too fast here. I heard about the cop that got shot. You should have just called me instead of playin' it like a Bruce Willis movie. I didn't have a fucking thing to do with what happened at the Hilton two days ago." Victor paused to examine his cigarette. He ordered Bernie to untie Arney's hands. Arney rubbed his wrists while trying to anticipate Victor's next move. Victor finished counting some cash and stuck it hastily into an old leather briefcase.

"Well amigo here's where we stand." He slowly circled Arney's chair. "You had the fucking nerve to invade my private domain armed with a deadly weapon and I just don't know what to think. What was on your mind hombre?" Victor scruffed Arney's hair.

"Were you gonna try and take me out?"

"…I just wanted to have a talk with you, shall we say, holding the aces."

Victor let out a howl. "Is that what you call it? I'd say that it would be more along the lines of a threatening interview designed to scare the shit out of me and maybe more." Victor looked over at the big 'B' and said, "escort our friend here gently back to the front gate and make sure he gets in his car and fastens his seat belt properly."

Then the mobster bent down to be eye to eye with his captive. "And you… mother fucker, you're still working for me whether you take my money or not. You've got just 48 hours to tell me what lock or locks those keys fit that I gave you." Victor stubbed out his latest cigarette. "Get this piece of shit out of my sight!"

The pair arrived at the gates. Bernie spoke, "You're a very lucky man Arney." The private eye swung around and karate chopped the big man in the windpipe. He smacked the sidewalk gasping for air.

Arney slid by the gate and stepped out. "That's okay 'B', I can find my way."

His head was throbbing as he headed back to Silver Lake to pull himself together. One thing was bothering him. Victor had kept his Colt. He'd have to let McCreary know in case his weapon showed up on the computer linked to a recent crime.

Arney was way pissed. He was beginning to think that grandfather Fick was hiding something and if the private eye with a throbbing headache was going to figure it out, a visit to Pasadena was due sooner than later.

And what about the mysterious keys which Victor put such emphasis on? Where did they come from and what lies behind the door or doors they open?

Thirteen

The crowd gathered in the banquet room of the Knickerbocker Hotel in New York was the cream of the elite in the art world. Collectors, dealers, agents and artists were there to honor the grand dame of twentieth century art restoration. Each felt privileged to be in the presence of the woman who had in her long career, saved millions of dollars worth of paintings, let alone the contribution of preserving our cultural history through her expertise.

Madeline Steinman, the eighty-seven year old with mischievous eyes, sipped her dry vodka martini in one of the conference rooms of the Hotel as she answered the T.V. journalist's questions on auto-pilot. The camera lights for the taped interview were making her irritable. She was tired and wanted to return to her suite and double bolt the doors.

An American ex-pat, she moved to Paris from New York and never looked back. The year was 1947 and the twenty-two year old accepted a job as one of several assistants to the head of art restoration at the Louvre. She arrived amidst turmoil and conflict as Europe was trying to piece itself back together after the war.

It was a little known fact that when the Mona Lisa was stolen in 1976 during viewer hours by two men dressed as janitors, that it was Madeline Steinman out of all of the experts available that was chosen to restore the icon after it was heavily damaged while in the possession of the thieves. Leonardo would have been proud.

But that type of notoriety would come later in her life and experience. Her formative years in Paris were full of impressions, places, and people. Within a few weeks of arriving she met the first man in her life that truly intrigued her. She could listen to him talk for hours, but he was interested in her thoughts as well. He encouraged her dreams and fueled her desire to restore the past for future generations.

Roderich Fick could sense the genius in her soul. He was a German hiding out from the authorities; an architect who had been singled out by Hitler to bring to reality the Fuehrer's visions of the future.

She was a Jew— he a Nazi. There was twenty years difference in their age. They fell madly in love: star-crossed lovers at their best.

Every night they met at a café tucked away on a secluded street in Montmartre. One evening Roderich brought a letter to show to Madeline.

He told her about his nephew and what he had done to secure the boy's future. The child's father had recently died and his mother, desperate without him went insane. The boy was on his own and alone in the world. Roderich begged Madeline to help him out. She vowed to do whatever was possible, not really knowing what that might be.

The TV interview came to a close. After a few insincere phrases of thanks to the press, she excused herself. There was time for a breath of fresh air before the evening began. She took her canes to find a quiet nook where she could be surrounded by silence. On the mezzanine floor there was a garden meditation room full of plants and flowers which was unoccupied. Madeline sat on a wooden bench surrounded by rose bushes and took a yellowed envelope out of her purse. She fondled the object gently then closed her eyes and pictured her lover's face all of those decades past. Inside the envelope was a letter. She read it with her eyes half-closed.

Mon. Ambroise Vollard November 21, 1926
43 rue de St. Germaine du pres.
Paris
My dearest Constantine,

I have had such a frightful day that I could not think of anyone but my precious sister to confide in about my troubles with the hopes that she may offer the compassion necessary for me to get through this ordeal. Mon Dieu~! Never in my life had I faced such a trial of patience let alone the monetary disaster that has befallen me which brings me near to contemplating suicide! I am not jesting.

As you know, for the past two years I have been handling in the capacity of a broker and manager the works of some of the Impressionists. Paul Cezanne has nearly driven me crazy because of his eccentric ways. He is completely unorganized and thinks nothing of leaving his paintings at bar/hotels in lieu of payments demanded by the proprietors of said establishments for his food and lodging. I have told him a thousand times to meet with me so that I may give him some sous before he wanders off to play the vagabond. Does he listen? Mais no!!! And then when he returns I have to trace his steps to backtrack to the bistros he frequented to pay the owners his debt and retrieve his small paintings. To date I have gathered over twenty of his sketches and oils from the region of the Var and Provence which has eaten up my time and my pocketbook.

Cher Constantine, alors! this is not the real problem I have need of communicating with you. No, my affairs with Cezanne are relatively easy in comparison with my association with Claude Monet.

I have just returned from the painter's home in Giverny. I believe that I wrote you several weeks back informing you that I had set up a gallery exhibition for Monet to expose thirteen of his new paintings in Paris. He was supposed to call me when he had completed the series. I had visited his studio as often as possible and his work was coming along wonderfully. I can't tell you how excited I was to be the one he trusted to organize and arrange the proceedings. It was to be in that gallery near the Gare de Lyons not far from the Opera. Do you remember it? I took you there to see Marie Cassette's water colors a few months ago.

Mon Dieu I am sweating profusely just telling you about this tragedy. Two days before I was to arrive with a cameo to pick up the paintings I called Monet and there was no answer. I tried again later in the day; the same. I then began to call every hour on the hour for nearly an entire day! Finally, I took the train to his studio, feeling an ominous emotion throughout the journey.

I disembarked at the station and ran all the way to his residence. Madame Monet, in her usual detached mood, told me that her husband was in the studio. Merci mon Dieu! I thought that he must be putting the finishing touches on the paintings. I ran across the bridge over the Japanese pond and tore into the studio. The master was seated at his table smoking one of his one hundred hand rolled cigarettes he consumes per day and there were two wine bottles perched near him; one empty, one half-empty. He did not acknowledge my presence. I gently spoke his name and within a few seconds he turned his head in my direction. As if I were a complete stranger he addressed me. "What are you doing here?"

I saddled up to his table dragging an old chair with me. "I'm here to collect your new series to take back to Paris for the exhibition that starts this weekend. You knew I was coming. We talked about it several times. What is the matter with you? Are you ill or something?"

Monet did not reply. He just continued to stare off into the far corner of the giant studio. I soon followed suit and to my shock my eyes discovered that all of the thirteen canvases had been slashed with a knife. I was dumbfounded. I became numb. I couldn't believe my eyes. I ran over to the pile of mutilated paintings and took each one in my hands trying to figure out why he had done such an insane thing so close to the showing? I looked back at him. He was still seated at the table smoking a fresh cigarette and sipping on his wine. I ran back and cried out one word. "Pourquoi?" It was impossible for me to understand his actions.

The big man stood up saying nothing to me and gathered up his tobacco and half-empty bottle of wine. He headed toward the door and paused before leaving. He turned to me and calmly spoke this phrase. "No damn good!"

He then asked me to put the paintings in the trash. He never wanted to see them again.

My dear sister, I am arriving at your home tomorrow morning, and with your kind permission, to store these ruined master works in your basement until I can figure out what to do. Please inform me without haste as to if this plan is not convenient for you.

With the dearest of regards and merciful thanks, your devoted brother
Ambroise

Madeline Steinman only stared at groups of words for she knew the letter by heart.

Because no one except Ambroise Vollard and his sister knew about these mysterious Monets, in the real world they didn't exist. The treasure for his nephew was well planned by Roderich: the boy could never be accused of stealing paintings which were unknown. These rare pieces of modern art were not confiscated by the Third Reich.

While folding the letter she pictured herself and Roderich, seated in their favorite café that cold April evening. She recalled the tale he told.

It was early in 1942 when the Fuehrer was planning the future. Hitler summoned Roderich to Berlin to discuss the museum project. The architect took the train from Stuttgart but stopped over-night in Hamburg to meet with one of the artists he had contracted for the project.

One thing Hitler ordered was a mural painted across the west wall of the interior depicting him as a modern day Zeus. The most talented of muralists in Germany at that time was Derek Ulbrect. Roderich assured the Fuehrer that there was no one more qualified. The painter's imagination was magical, unearthly. Roderich stopped in Hamburg to pick up Derek's proposed designs.

Ulbrect met him at the train and with much excitement he began to talk about a woman who had shown up at his favorite café claiming to have in her hotel room, thirteen mutilated canvases of Claude Monet. Derek had insisted that they go there immediately to hear her story.

Roderich was tired but knew his stubborn friend well. Besides, he was starving, and thought perhaps there would be some food left at this late hour.

They arrived fifteen minutes later to find the café nearly empty and the woman asleep in one of the booths. Derek asked the proprietor what happened. Where is everyone?

The owner who was washing up told them that the old whore was bothering everyone for wine and then all of the sudden she passed out.

Roderich asked for two sandwiches and a couple of beers and went over to where the old woman was resting.

Derek gave him the key to his apartment. He laughed as he warned Roderich to be careful; she was not to be trusted. Roderich woke up the old woman and offered her a sandwich and a beer. She lunged at both.

It turns out that she had been the parlor maid of Constantine Vollard, the sister of a famous art dealer in Paris. This pitiful creature who called herself Camille claimed that she had been falsely accused of stealing from her employer and was fired without a reference or any severance pay. She had heard her mistress discussing the mutilated works of the famous painter that were in the basement. She packed them along with her personal belongings and escaped to Germany. She was never caught.

Until that very night, when her drunkenness got the better of her, she had kept the secret of the missing Monets to herself, hoping some day to cash in.

She led Roderich back to her hovel and showed him the paintings along with the letter written from Ambroise to his sister. He offered her three thousand francs for the thirteen discarded Monets and the letter. She eagerly accepted. She rolled up the heavy canvases and placed them into a straw basket, continuing to babble. Roderich became more anxious to leave. She was definitely senile and half out of her mind.

Madeline remembered the last thing he did before he disappeared from her life forever. He gave her the letter she now held tightly in her hands. "This was written by Ambroise Vollard to his sister. I want you to have it—keep it to remember me by."

A couple entered the garden room animated in conversation. Madeline's reverie was broken. She pulled herself up on her canes and headed back for the banquet room. As she approached the entrance she pictured that day one year later in 1948 when a scared teenage boy arrived with a valise full of torn canvases at her apartment in Paris—a teenaged Ezekiel Fick.

It was the one unscrupulous act of a lifetime: her private project of deception. She recalled the pure labor of love as she meticulously restored Monet's lost works with a passion that was never surpassed in her life's work.

Madeline Steinman requested one of the reworked Monet canvases as her fee. It was a portrait of an unknown man. She kept it hidden away in her apartment in Paris. Every now and then she took it out. The gentle face depicted on the canvas reminded her of Roderich.

Fourteen

Things were spinning out of control and it was time to gather up all the facts and total the damage. Arney needed a plan.

He wandered out to his car to get the envelope Victor gave him. Glancing across the street at the lake, his eyes drifted along the blue-green water's rippling motion. A Santa Ana was on the way.

Out of habit, he shot a look up and down Silver Lake Boulevard and spotted a dark sedan about a block and a half away occupied by two suits: these two were probably not parked by the lake to enjoy a snack and hold hands. His instinct said they were tailing him, possibly undercover — maybe two of Victor's boys.

Arney ambled back into his house and dumped the contents of the envelope, including the slip of paper handed to him at the hospital on his dining table then looked down the street from his front bay window to see if the car was still there.

It was gone.

He went to the kitchen and ground some fresh Colombian coffee beans while placing three chocolate chip cookies on a plate. While the water boiled, he grabbed a legal pad. With his coffee cup in his right hand and a cookie in his left, he knew he was ready for some serious thinking.

The phone rang. It was his contact at Ma Bell telling him that the number handed to him at the hospital was a disposable cell phone, untraceable. He hung up and ate a cookie.

Mid second cookie the phone rang again. Arney looked at the number display; it was the same as he had on the paper. He waited for three rings then picked up. No greetings were necessary. "Who are you and what do you have to tell me?"

There was a hissing pause then a woman's voice. "*It was a mistake...*" The same phrase as on the note. The voice was middle-aged.

Arney jumped down her throat. "...A mistake? You're telling me that shooting my friend was a mistake? What in the hell do you have to do with this—are you one of Victor's people?"

The phone went dead, then came a light tapping on the front door. He peeked around the bay window curtains but could only make out a rather nicely shaped rear end attached to the body of a small female. He threw open the door and startled his visitor. She dropped a small bag which made a hard clunking sound when it landed on the brick porch. It was Victor's girl, Conchita Morales. "...Uh, mister Victor asked me to return this to you." She bent down to retrieve the sack, her breasts almost tumbling out of her blouse.

Arney looked in the plastic bag but already knew by the weight that it was his Colt 9m.

With no particular motive in mind he said, "...Feel like a cup of coffee? I've got Colombian beans...grind 'em on the spot." Conchita agreed shyly and stepped inside. He moved ahead of her quickly clearing his evidence off the dining table then offered her a chair. She sat with her hands folded in her lap as if she were attending church. Arney kept an eye out as he ground the beans and set the kettle. He returned to the table with a small platter of chocolate chip cookies. She laughed when she saw it. She lit a cigarette without asking permission. "So, the big-time macho private eye is a cookie monster?" She giggled again.

Arney smiled as he returned with the coffee cups and a French press.

"Sorry to disappoint, I'm not very tall either."

She threw a confused look at him. "What's that got to do with it?"

Arney replied, "Nothing…it's just a line from an old Bogart movie."

"Who…?" She asked.

"Forget it." He was feeling his age. He poured the coffee then looked into her eyes. They were large and almond colored, really setting off her face and her light brown skin.

"Feel like talking?" He said as he toasted her with his cup in the air.

She took a sip mulling over the question. "I'm just a working girl—I don't have much to say." She began to get nervous. Her eyes darted round the room.

Arney tried to lighten the atmosphere. "Did you know about the lake right across the street before you came here today?"

She gazed out of his bay window at the man-made body of water and casually remarked, "Sure. The north end is a good spot to turn a trick. I'll bet someone is getting a blow job right now while you and I are here having coffee and cookies." She burst out laughing and Arney joined her.

"Sorry about that. For a moment I forgot how you earn your keep. Pretty stupid of me."

The twenty-something Latina hooker reached over and tenderly touched Arney's thigh. "It's okay man, I appreciate the fact that you forgot. You're a sweet guy."

With that, she stood up and slung her purse over her shoulder. "Thanks for the snack. I'll tell Victor you were home when I stopped by."

Arney followed her to the front door. "Just one question if you don't mind." Conchita paused. "A little while before you arrived there were two guys in a new sedan parked down the street. I think they were watching me. Would you know if they were Victor's boys?"

Conchita smiled. "I don't know much, my man, but if it was a new sedan it would not be from Victor's crew. He's only into vintage cars; sixties and seventies." She reached into her purse to find her car keys. "He likes his cars old and fast and his women young and faster." She offered a small wave and scurried down the street.

He went back inside without following her with his eyes.

———— ◆ ————

P.I. Blackburn sat with the evidence bag, legal pad and a fresh cup of coffee. The mysterious keys clattered on the table top. He picked them up and put on his reading glasses. They looked identical but one had a series of eight numbers imprinted above the blade near the brand name: 77867432 Schlage.

He took out his little black book and skimmed through until he found Marty's lock and key in Riverside. Marty had done time for grand-theft-auto ten years ago. When he was released Arney helped him get a fresh start as a locksmith. The irony still made him smile.

Within ten minutes the detective knew a little more than when he started his day. Marty told him that Schlage, the key manufacturer relegated their serial numbers to regions of every state they were in. Seven was California and seventy eight was Long Beach. Arney went up on his laptop and located eleven lock and key shops in the area. This was not going to be detective fun. It was only five o'clock. He would have time to call the shops before they closed to see if there was anything to be gained.

Another knock at the door.

Arney didn't look out the window this time. He figured it was Conchita.

Wrong.

He turned the knob and the door flew open, slamming him against the wall. He recognized the two suits from the car he'd seen earlier. No time to react. They pounded the crap out of him in less than thirty seconds. Arney felt a rib snap.

The two muscles paused over his writhing body and one of them said, "This is just our way of saying lay off the Fick case. You're not a cop anymore." They slammed the door and Arney passed out curled up in fetal position on the entryway tiles.

Unlike the movies, you don't always wake up from a good beating and wonder where you are. Blackburn knew right where he was and exactly what had happened. He sat up and leaned against the entrance wall. His rib cage was killing him. There was a rap on the front door and he heard his neighbor Dr. Tom call out. "Arney, you okay?"

He managed to open the door. Tom stepped in to access the damage.

"Geez, you took a hell of a beating. Looks like the hit you took at the Silver Lake Silverfish ball game last year."

Arney groaned as the doctor checked his ribs. "Yeah, I didn't see this one coming."

Tom was gently pressing his rib cage. "Well I spied those two defensive ends that ran out of your house a little while ago. I was on my porch taking a few photos of the garden. Don't know if it will do any good but I grabbed a shot of their license plate as they sped away. Thought it would be a good idea to come over and see if you were still breathing."

Dr. Tom tightened an Ace bandage around the detective's ribs and he let out a yelp. "There, that should hold you. Take it off when you shower, but don't shower until tomorrow. Here's that plate number and a few pain pills to hold you over in the meantime." The doctor smiled. "Give me a call if you need me, and do me a favor—pick your playmates with more discretion. I'm going on vacation next week for ten days. Get my drift?"

Arney thanked Dr. Tom while shaking his hand. The click of the front door closing was a cue to head for the bed. What in the hell was going on? Was Stephanie Fick still alive? Had her captors been torturing her? He was aching from head to toe but he couldn't get his mind off of the victim. He pulled the blanket over him and felt Dr. Tom's pills kicking in. Soon he was off the radar.

When he woke up it was dark. It didn't matter what time it was. He was coming out of the fog. He popped two more of the pain pills Dr. Tom gave him and realized how much his ribs were killing him.

The incident with the two suits and his current physical condition was focusing him. First there was the shooting of Gary Bub, then the failed attempt to shake-down Victor Gastaldi and now this; beaten to shit on his own doorstep. Enough is enough: time to clean house.

Arney checked the clock in the kitchen while grabbing a cookie. It was two a.m. He took out the piece of paper Dr. Tom had written down the license number on. They were county plates. That means that someone with influence had it in for him. The bruised and battered private eye was tempted to wake up Chief Mac but it would hold until tomorrow.

Did Ezekiel Fick have something to do with this? Was he calling the shots?

Arney went over to the mirror to take a look at his face. He had a black eye and cut on his cheek that Dr. Tom had treated without him being aware of it. There was no time like the present. He was sure that the Pasadena billionaire would welcome him with open arms at three in the morning.

Fifteen

Ezekiel Fick's mansion was in the heart of San Marino, the most upscale section of Pasadena. Arney had no trouble finding it.

The estate loomed behind a tall wrought-iron fence with a video camera/voice box mounted on a pole at the entrance. Arney hit the buzzer and held it down for five seconds. An angry voice answered. "Yes, what is it?"

Arney smiled as he responded. "Private detective Arnold Blackburn here, I need to talk to Mr. Fick about the kidnapping of his granddaughter. I'm afraid that it won't wait until tomorrow." That line usually did the trick. The gate buzzed open.

At ten miles an hour, it took nearly a minute for him to arrive at the front door. Waiting for him on the porch in a pair of silk pajamas and a velvet robe which probably cost more than Arney used to make in a month on the force, was the elder Fick . Arney breezed past him into the mansion. "Nice place you've got here, a little big for my tastes, but livable just the same."

The old man was boiling. "Just who in the fuck are you and what do you know about Stephanie's kidnapping?"

Arney turned around and stood with his face mere inches from Fick's. "Oh, I think you know who I am and why I'm here. It's time to cut the bullshit Fick. In the past week I nearly lost one of my best friends and I've been pummeled in my own house. And you know what? It's all because of you and your precious granddaughter." The old man peered over Arney's shoulder. "Oh yes and you can tell your stooge that if he comes within ten feet of me he won't be walking for a very long time—maybe never again." The look on the P.I.'s face was convincing.

The old man waved off whoever was standing behind him. "Follow me."

Arney's ribs were killing him but he didn't let on. They entered a room with more square footage than his house in Silver Lake. Fick offered Arney a whisky and he took it. He needed something to wash down two more pain pills.

He moved right along. "Where is she?"

The old man looked as if he was listening to a foreign language. "What in the hell do you mean? How should I know where she is? I've got the whole goddamn world looking for her as we speak."

Arney downed his whisky and went over and poured himself another. "Well, if you don't know where she is, then you certainly know why she was kidnapped and it wasn't for a ransom. That little item has failed to show up." Arney stirred the ice cubes with his finger. "So why don't you tell me what was in the package you ran off with the other night from Griffith Park?" Fick started to interrupt but Arney waved him off. "Don't go there old man. I was sitting on the lawn right across from you when you reached behind the bench after the phone call." Fick's shoulders slumped. Arney waited for the old man to gather his thoughts.

"Do you have a past, detective?"

Arney shrugged.

"Of course you do. We all do." The billionaire poured himself a tumbler and continued.

"When were you born? My guess would be somewhere in the 1970's, am I correct?"

Arney nodded.

Ezekiel chuckled. "Young man, long before you were born the world was a much different place than it is today. There was no technology in the hands of the masses and things moved much slower; time passed quietly. The word stress was seldom uttered.

"My uncle knew that my father was gravely ill and that he would not live very much longer. At the end of World War II, I collected thirteen unknown, partially destroyed canvases rendered by a great French Impressionist. No one was aware of their existence except his agent. They were slashed with a knife by the artist after completing them before a scheduled showing around nineteen twenty-six. His agent stored them away instead of taking them to the trash as the painter had requested. I never knew how my uncle ended up with them. The last time I talked with him he directed me to a friend of his in Paris who was an art restoration genius. I took them to her in nineteen forty-eight and she repaired them. The monies I derived from these restored works gave me the capital to invest. I made a fortune. My uncle sealed my fate long before I was aware of it."

Arney listened like a cocked hammer ready to go off. "And why in the hell should anyone believe all of this bullshit about discarded masterpieces? Maybe you're just a good story teller. What proof do you have about this life of yours? How can I know you're telling the truth?"

Fick kicked off his slippers and settled into the couch. Arney poured another whisky realizing he was in for the long haul.

"I was born in Germany but grew up in Switzerland as a teenager during World War II. My parents moved to a remote area in the mountains after Hitler invaded Poland. We lived quietly in a neutral country.

"At that time, Hitler was gathering huge amounts of ancient art treasures. He believed that many of these objects were blessed with secret powers invested by the artists themselves. Hitler's belief in the Occult is well documented. His fascination with the Supernatural dominated his life." The old man paused to scrutinize Arney for a few seconds. He was debating over just how much he was willing to divulge. "Hitler needed an incredible museum to house all of his treasures when the war ended." Fick paused to look up. "My uncle was Roderich Fick. Does that name mean anything to you?"

Arney shook his head relieved that the pain pills were starting to kick in.

"He was a great architect. Adolph Hitler engaged him to build a museum in Austria. When Germany surrendered my uncle disappeared. I never saw him again. But once, during the war, he visited us at our chalet in the mountains above Lausanne." Fick set down his drink and rubbed his eyes. "He gave me an envelope telling me not to open it until my father passed away. Papa died shortly after the war ended."

Arney interrupted. "So, who was the mysterious artist who tried to destroy his own paintings?" Arney's ribs were beginning to ache again. "And why in the hell should anyone buy this fairy tale crap about living out the Second World War in a forest cottage?"

The old man chuckled. "I don't blame you for feeling that way Mr. Blackburn and perhaps at some other time I'll reveal the name of the artist but for now..." Fick glanced at the clock on the mantle. "I'll tell you one thing. I've done nothing illegal or wrong. Whoever has kidnapped my poor Stephanie has made a huge mistake."

Arney sat up straight waiting for the pay-off but Fick stopped short.

"It's late and I need to sleep. I haven't had much since Stephanie was taken from me."

Arney stood up. "Well and fine Zeke, but you still haven't told me why you think there hasn't been a ransom note. Does it have to do with something else your uncle left for you? Did he leave you a fortune in art treasures confiscated from the Jews and tucked away during the war?"

Ezekiel Fick stared off into space. "As I've just told you, my uncle left me a treasure of rare modern art." Ezekiel Fick was beyond fatigue. "These paintings had never been seen by anyone because technically, they didn't exist. There was no record of them and they were not stolen from the Jews or any museum in Europe." Fick glanced again at the clock again, put his slippers back on and began to slowly rise to his feet. He gave Arney a blank stare.

Arney stood up. "And that's all you have to say to me? You can't be more specific? You aren't willing to share the content of the package you picked up in the park?"

Fick smiled. "Not in my own house without my attorney present. Besides, you're not officially the police are you? Anything I've said here tonight in front of you, even if you've secretly recorded it, is inadmissible evidence." The old man escorted Arney to the door. "Find her

Blackburn... find her and I'll make it more than worth your time and trouble."

Arney took out his car keys and jangled them. "Oh, I'll find her, but if you continue with this secret bullshit routine, she might not be breathing when I do."

Sixteen

The sun peeked over the San Gabriel Mountains as Arney drove down Orange Grove Boulevard in the early morning hours. After listening for over an hour to Ezekiel Fick's life story he was no further along than he was the day before. But maybe, just maybe Fick was trying to tell him something. Read between the lines Blackburn, read between the lines.

Arney cautiously opened his front door to the sound of his home phone ringing.

It was Chief Mac. "Jesus Christ Arney, where in the hell have you been? I tried your cell a dozen times."

The tired detective jumped in. "I have a much better question than yours. Who in the fuck sent two of L.A.'s finest to my house yesterday to warn me off this case while cracking a couple of my ribs?"

Chief Mac was silent.

"Oh, so you do know." The battered detective waited for a response.

The old man spoke in a low voice. "Listen my friend, I had nothing to do with it. There are powers above mine that are keenly interested in this case for reasons other than the kidnapping itself."

Arney grabbed the last chocolate chip cookie from yesterday's batch. "Well I've just returned from the Fick residence where Ezekiel and I spent the wee hours of the morning downing malt whisky and discussing Adolph Hitler's love of fine art. I think I know why the potential heiress was kidnapped and why there hasn't been a ransom note. A sack full of money wouldn't cover her return fare."

Chief Mac sounded out of breath. "What did you just say? You spent the night with Fick and he told you that he was a Nazi? I don't believe it."

Arney walked into the kitchen for a sip of milk. "No, I didn't say *he* was a Nazi nor did he claim to be one. He's of German descent but his father moved the family to Switzerland when Hitler invaded Poland. On the other hand, Fick's uncle was one of Hitler's preferred architects. The Fuehrer and his crew grabbed most of the fine art of Western Europe between nineteen-forty and forty-five. Uncle Roderich was supposed to build the ultimate museum in Austria to house all of Hitler's stash. With the German surrender that project was never to be, yet, there were still hundreds of vaults containing all of these priceless treasures strewn around Europe.

"Fick's uncle was looking out for him. He gave him an envelope which Fick was to open after his father died. I'm not sure when Fick's father passed away but in forty-eight the young Fick took a bundle of unknown Impressionist paintings his uncle left him to an art expert in Paris to have them restored. The Fick fortune was not just industrials. That came later." Arney gulped down his milk. "I'm starting to believe that when Ezekiel Fick turned eighteen he had the potential to make millions of dollars with paintings created by a famous artist which no one knew about."

McCreary sighed. "That would explain it."

Arney quipped. "Explain what?"

Fergus spoke in his official voice. "You'd better come down to headquarters as soon as possible. I'll have breakfast waiting for you in my office. See you in an hour." The phone went dead before Arney had a chance to respond.

Arney was surprised by the quality of his breakfast. The whole time he was munching away Chief Mac gathered files, sorting through them at his desk. He looked up.

"…More coffee?"

Better service than Denny's. Arney slurped down the last sips of his cup. "Nope, I'm fine. Can we get along with it now?"

Mac got up and sat on the corner of his desk. "Have you ever heard of the ARCA?" The private-eye shook his head. "Well the initials stand for the Association into the Research of Crimes against Art. A British judge named Arthur Tomkins is one of their leaders. While attending an Interpol convention he connected with some of the members of the stolen arts division which eventually led to his association with ARCA."

Arney stood up and began to pace. "So these ARCA people also believe that Fick has a stash of stolen art and they kidnapped Stephanie to force his hand?"

Fergus returned to his chair. "No, I've spoken with Tomkins on the phone. I don't think a public organization such as ARCA would commit a crime to justify revenge."

Chief Mac paused for a moment to think . "… But I might not be too far off-base to think that there might be a few members within the organization whose families were persecuted during World War II who may have decided to take the law into their own hands."

Arney laughed. "…You serious Chief?"

Mac nodded. "I not only think that, but I know it for a fact." A shy expression came over the old lawman. "I believe that what happened to you yesterday was instigated by people in very high standing around Hollywood. Those two who worked you over were not our boys. They were just using our transportation."

Arney sat back down and let out a sigh. "So where does that leave us? What good am I to this whole scene?"

McCreary stared at the top of his desk. "You might just be our best chess piece. Victor Gastaldi has got something to do with this and I know it. Stolen works of art are great exchanges for drugs and arms. One priceless painting would finance a drug cartel or outfit an army in the Mid-East or Central America for years, maybe forever."

Arney was beginning to see the whole picture. "So you want me to continue my game with Gastaldi and see where it goes?"

"That would be a good idea." The lawman smiled. "And anything else you can think of that might be useful."

Arney returned to Silver Lake down Sunset Boulevard from the Second Street underpass. He wanted to get home and research the mysterious keys Victor Gastaldi had given him.

Also, an old contact from the film industry might have something to contribute to the pot: with leftovers you make a stew.

Seventeen

On the north side of Sunset Boulevard in the heart of Beverly Hills, set back in the winding maze of white-cement streets are some of the priciest homes on the planet. Many have had the same owners for decades dating back to the end of the Second World War. One such residence sits nestled in a small forest. Even for Beverly Hills this is rare. No one could even guess the price of this location.

The owner never thinks about that. He's going nowhere until the day he stops breathing. He is eighty three years old and that day is closer than it was yesterday.

Abraham Meyers was the son of the Baron Solomon Misha Meyers, the Hungarian art collector whose entire collection was confiscated by the Nazis and the Hungarian government during the war.

Meyers is one of the most important personalities in the history of the Hollywood film industry. Until his retirement three years ago, he was the most influential agent in the business. He'd handled everyone from Marlon Brando to Dustin Hoffman and Meryl Streep and all of those in between. The first name you thought of when getting ready to cast was Abraham Meyers. Everyone else was second in line.

Abe Meyers had been involved for over four decades with various organizations concerned with the recovery of stolen and confiscated works of art for the Jewish people and their families. The final goal of his life is to have all of his father's collection returned to him by the Hungarian government and the museums which currently house the works.

His friend Hillary Clinton was successful in getting the ball rolling contributing to a landmark decision by the US commission on security and co-operation in the EU. Legislation was passed which would speed up the process of returning the stolen works of art to their original owners. She had recently called Abe to tell him that a portion of the over one hundred works of art that were confiscated by the Nazis from his father during the war which included paintings by Valesquez, Renoir, Monet, El Greco, Corot, and Vandyke would soon be with him.

He was sipping his favorite tea while browsing through the Hollywood Reporter when his butler arrived with the phone.

"...A Mr. Blackburn on the line for you, sir."

Abe Meyers grabbed the phone, surprised. "Arney, it's been a long time. How in the hell have you been?"

Arney stopped by Cedars to visit Bub on his way to see Abe Meyers. He crept into the room thinking his friend was asleep.

"Jesus, I hope you didn't bring me a fucking doughnut."

Arney laughed. "No, but when you're back on the street I'm taking you to In and Out, my treat."

Bub tried to turn a little bit in his bed. "Music to my ears Blackburn."

Arney pulled up a chair. "I can't tell you how sorry I am..."

Bub waved him off. "Listen dude, it was my own fault. I should've been more careful." Bub took a sip of water.

Arney waited. "What the hell happened?"

The shot-up cop closed his eyes. "Right after I hung up with you, I saw someone with a handgun heading towards the ladies john, couldn't tell if it was a man or a woman. I ran over to see what was going on but I didn't draw my gun. The toilet looked empty. I turned around to leave and then I heard the pop of a silencer. I knew I was going to be hit and down I went."

"Did you see who did it?"

Bub let out a groan. "I wish I had. I'm not even sure that I could ID the person I followed. Funny thing was that it must have been a woman even though I wasn't sure at first."

Arney followed up. "….Because they went into the ladies head?"

"Roger, copy that. I don't think a cop has ever been shot by a dude in the ladies powder room. I'll have to check up on that when they kick me out of here."

Arney put his hands behind his head. "When do you think that'll happen?"

Bub searched for a more comfortable position in bed. "They're talking about this weekend, but I won't be back on the job for about a couple of months. I'll need some rehab for the arm."

Arney was about to break into another apology when Bub jumped in. "So, I guess that'll give us a couple of weeks to wrap this case up."

Arney smiled. "You mean…"

"I mean I want the son-of-a-bitch who did this who also probably kidnapped the girl. You keep the doughnuts coming, I'm there."

Arney got up. "Call me when you're heading home I'll stop by to make sure you've got what you need. The wounded cop saluted his friend as the nurse arrived. Visiting hours were over.

Turning off of Sunset Blvd towards the Meyers' residence, Arney reviewed the incident that brought them together in the first place.

The ex-cop had saved the life of Abe's son in a nightclub on Wilshire five years ago. Arney had been searching the area of south Beverly Hills for a robbery suspect. He ducked in and out of all the bars in the vicinity of Beverly Boulevard and Wilshire. When he popped into the Eagles Nest on Robertson he caught three men pounding the shit out of another.

The victim couldn't be more than twenty-five years old and his assailants were an older crew dishing it out heavily. Arney stepped in and began to even the odds without disclosing that he was a representative of the law. In his experience he found that telling the bad guys he was the police somehow took all the fun out of it. He preferred to dive in first and announce his status later.

Arney took the man who was whacking the shit of the youngster with a pool cue and pinned him against the wall jamming the cue stick into his nuts. That more than slowed him down. The other two, taking notice of the new guy paused just long enough for Arney to flash his smile along with his badge. He told the bartender to call 911 and cuffed the suspects to the legs of the pool table. He was just in time. The victim, Abraham Meyers junior was rushed to the hospital in critical condition but managed to survive and eventually returned to full health.

Abe senior was more than thankful and invited him to his home where he offered Arney a sizeable check. The lieutenant detective turned it down, but said that one day he might need a favor. Would a rain check work? The old man grinned and said, "You've got carte blanche, anytime Blackburn. Just give me a buzz."

Abraham Meyers had aged quite a bit in the five years since Arney had last seen him. His smile, however, was still warm and full of honest joy. He was a man you could feel comfortable around. After a drink on the veranda, they retired to the library and shut the doors. The old man sat back in his easy chair and said, "Well Arney, what can I do you for?"

Arney smiled. "How's your son?"

The old man downed another cognac. "My boy married about a year after you saved his life. He's living in Hawaii with his wife and two children. Believe it or not, he owns a surf shop for Christ's sake. Can you imagine a Jew surfer in the family? I couldn't, but it's all worked out very well. He's happy and that's all a father can ask for of his children." Abe Meyers put his hands behind his head and leaned back. "I appreciate your concern, but that's not why you're here. I understand that you are no longer one of L.A.'s finest."

Arney grinned. "You checked up on me after I called?"

"I was just curious about your current position in life. Wanted to make sure you were okay. You, my boy, are like family. How's the private eye business?"

Arney stood up and stretched. "Glad you asked, Abe. That's why I'm here. Have you heard about the kidnapping of Ezekiel Fick's granddaughter?"

Abe took a pipe and some tobacco out his desk drawer. "Believe it or not, I haven't been in the business for over three years and I'm getting calls from some idiot screen writer who wants my advice on a treatment of this tragedy. Show business gets uglier every day." Abe lit up. "Why in the hell did you come to me on this one?"

Arney laid his cards on the table. "This case isn't following the norm. There hasn't been a ransom note. Do you know anything about Ezekiel Fick?"

Abe blew out some smoke. "Just that he is one of the richest sons of a bitches in California. He's Swiss, right?"

"Right. But his uncle was Roderich Fick the architect who…"

Abe cut Arney off. "…The Nazi bastard who was going to build the Fuermuseum in Austria at the end of the war to house all Hitler stole from my people, including my own goddamn family!" Abe turned red. "May the bastard fry in hell."

Arney wasn't sure what to say next. Abe calmed down quickly and the smile returned to his face. This time, however, it was not his warm, caring smile; it was a pure Hollywood-deal-maker grin. "He told you didn't he?"

Arney tried to distance himself a little for safety's sake. "Told me what?"

Abe clapped his hands. "I thought so! Fick made off with a bundle of artwork after the War and it's here… in our own backyard?"

Arney was losing control. "Abe, no one knows that for sure. His granddaughter is captive somewhere in southern California and right now I'm helping the department to try and rescue her. I was hoping that you might provide me with some information I need."

Abraham Myers was staring at the ceiling with his fingers interlaced. He was far off in thought. He motioned for Arney to come over to where he was seated. As he moved towards him, Abe unbuttoned his shirt sleeve and rolled it up. When Arney arrived he saw the Auschwitz numbered tattoo on Abe's left forearm.

"Six months of my life I spent there, watching my people being tortured to death. That type of experience goes beyond memory. It sleeps with you, wakes up with you and follows you around all day long." Abe rolled down his sleeve. "I'm afraid my friend, as much as I owe you for saving Abe junior that I can be of no help to you in this matter. You can ask me for anything else and your wish will be granted, but I won't lift a finger to help you find Ezekiel Fick's granddaughter."

CHAPTER EIGHTEEN

Eighteen

Now what?

Arney headed home with this thought spinning around in his head. He drove east on Sunset intending to head up Cahuenga and grab the 101 back to Silver Lake but decided to cruise Sunset.

This was one lousy week. Why in the hell did he tell Chief McCrary that he'd be able to handle this case? Jesus, so far he hadn't scored a touchdown and on every play he was being pushed back behind the scrimmage line. The old saying was ringing true: no good deed goes unpunished.

At Fairfax, Arney took a right feeling more like driving on Santa Monica Boulevard. While stopped at the light he gazed across the street at a florist shop. A young girl wearing an apron was watering plants and arranging the pots outdoors with a big smile. This would be a fun life. Why didn't he think about doing something else? There's dozens of private detectives in L.A. What makes him so special? Is it the fact that he can't do anything right?

On the border of launching into an extravaganza of self-pity, his cell went off. It was the mystery woman. He pulled over. He said nothing waiting for her, whoever she was, to talk.

Silence.

He thought he'd lost her and was about to hang up when she spoke. "Can we meet?"

"…Where?"

"There's a little café in Venice on Lincoln near the corner of seventh. It's called Vienna. Can we hook up there in an hour?"

Arney paused to think it over. He didn't need another pounding. "How will I know you?"

The voice answered. "I'll find you. I've seen your picture in the paper."

Arney hadn't checked out the L.A. Times for several days. There must have been a photo of him around the time Gary Bub was shot. "See you in an hour."

The private detective closed his phone with a hundred questions dancing around on his windshield.

He was ten minutes from home. He could shower, change and be in Venice a few minutes ahead of schedule. When he turned the corner he spotted a limo parked in front of his house. The driver was standing on the sidewalk holding an envelope. He handed it to the detective with the compliments of Abe Meyers, gave a stiff salute and drove off.

Arney opened it and took out one sheet of paper. It was a list of fourteen names. A post-it was attached. "Sorry for this afternoon. Hope this will help. Abe." He read the list in disbelief: a collection of some of the most prominent directors, actors, screenwriters and producers in Hollywood today. Every individual was a household name except for one. A woman named Madeline Steinman. Arney paused but no bells went off.

What prompted the old man to do an about-face in the last half hour? What did Abe's list have to do with the kidnapping? Were these persons part of ARCA? Were they some kind of vigilante organization? Were they responsible for the kidnapping?

Things were getting more confusing by the minute. He still hadn't taken the time to follow up on the keys Victor had given him. Before leaving he reached into a drawer near the TV and took out his hand gun. Right now it was time to meet the mystery woman of Venice.

He cruised by the café twice, before parking down the block and ambling back. It was only five in the afternoon and the coffee house was almost empty. Sitting at a corner booth was a woman about forty years of age with masculine features. She motioned him to join her. Arney sat with his back to the wall. She was dressed in jeans and a denim jacket. Her head was shaved and several piercings were scattered over her body. A large tattoo on her left bicep read *Dine on Mom*. She wore dark sunglasses. "Thanks for coming down."

Arney nodded.

She cleared her throat. "I don't know where to begin."

He sat up straight and leaned into her face. "Why don't we start with why you shot a cop and then decided to tell me about it?"

She tightened up. "I didn't shoot no fucking cop. But I know who did and it was a mistake. They were after another dude who looked like him." She backed away from the table and stood up. "I don't know why in the hell I called you, I'm outta here."

Arney pointed to the table top. "Sit down and tell me what you know. If you aren't involved with the actual crime you don't have anything to worry about." He took out his Iphone and snapped her picture. Then he picked up the glass of water she was drinking, tossed the liquid into a planter and carefully put the glass in his coat pocket. "There, that's all I need to find you. Can I buy you a cup of coffee?"

She smiled and sat back down. "It's just that my best friend got herself into a mess and that's how she shot the cop instead of the prick who was trying to fuck with her brother. You see, her brother is a big time drug dealer and..."

Arney interrupted her. "Whoa...would you mind starting at the beginning? First of all what's your name?"

The woman stared at the table-top. "Gail, Gail Goodman."

"Great Gail, now tell me who your friend is and who is this brother you're talking about? If I'm going to help you, and I think that's why you called me, I need to know all the details. I'm not asking you to trust me, but now that I'm here, I don't think you've got much of a choice."

Gail took a deep breath. "Okay. My friend is the sister of Victor Gastaldi. You ever heard of him?" Arney nodded. "He's pretty much got the town sewn up for drugs and high percentage loans which he calls in with a crew of scumbags. I've told Dee Dee a thousand times to get as far away from him as possible."

Arney cut in. "Victor has a sister named Dee Dee?"

The woman realized she'd just given out the name. "Fuck. I wasn't going to tell you her name."

Arney took a sip of coffee. "Tell me something. Why did you get in touch with me?"

She looked around nervously before replying. "I found out that you and the cop were friends, and that you were no longer a cop. I didn't know what else to do. I'm worried about Dee."

Arney was beginning to clear away the fog. "So, Dee Dee decided to off some dude that was moving in on her brother's rackets, so she went to the Hilton and shot the police officer thinking that he was this guy... Right?" The detective now knew how Danny Ballantyne fit into the picture.

Gail kept checking the front door. "That's only part of it. I think she's involved in a hell of a mess that might bring her down for good." She started to cry.

Arney was tempted to pat her on the shoulder but thought the better of it. "Just what kind of mess are we talking about here?"

She wiped her eyes with a napkin. "You heard about that missing Pasadena chick?"

Arney stayed calm. "Yeah, I've heard about it, so what?"

Gail let out a sigh. "I think Dee has something to do with her disappearance. Christ, she may even be one of the kidnappers. She's never at her apartment when I pass by and when I've caught her on her cell she says she's taking care of a friend. That's bullshit!"

"Why, doesn't she have any friends?"

"Dee and I have been lovers for three years now. I know all her friends. I checked with each of them. They haven't heard from her in over three weeks. She told me about a month ago that she had a big job coming up. I thought it was at the motorcycle shop she works at in Glendale. I called her boss two days ago and he hasn't seen her in weeks."

Arney was debating what to do next. He needed to tell McCreary about this new development. With Gail's photo and fingerprints on the glass he wouldn't have a problem finding her. There wasn't much else that Dee Dee's lover could tell him. She already spilled her guts out and her information was helping to connect the dots.

Time was wasting. He needed to find out what locks were waiting for those keys Victor gave him. He'd put that off long enough.

Arney asked Gail if she'd had a phone call recently from Dee. The answer was no. He stood up. "Here's my card with my land-line number also. If Dee Dee contacts you, call me, either at home or on my cell. I can't help you unless you stay in touch."

He left a Jackson for the coffee and headed back to his car wondering if he'd ever hear from her again.

Nineteen

Tunis was boiling at thirty-five degrees Celsius. Just outside the capital of Tunisia, Howard Solomon, the fifty-three year old four-time Academy Award winning film director tried to stay cool sucking on a frozen bottle of Coca-Cola.

His khaki shorts, shirt and cap with ear flaps were soaked through with sweat. The exclusive designer wrap-around sun glasses were dripping and fogged up: He could barely see the shot he was trying to film. The actors were irritable. The crew was ready to revolt, and after being on location for three weeks they were already two weeks behind schedule.

It was one o'clock and they had been at it since dawn. He called a lunch break and headed for his air-conditioned trailer. Right now Academy Awards meant nothing. His head was about to explode. He'd had a bad feeling about this project from the very beginning. Trying to back out of the contract was a no-go. He was stuck here for the duration and today his leading lady had a case of diarrhea that wouldn't go away.

Things couldn't be better.

But just to add to the mix, one night at the Sundance Film festival six months ago, an old high-school buddy from Chicago showed up. They ran into each other at the Pioneer bar and at first it was old home week. Howard had forgotten all about Danny B. They were pals in those days but had not stayed in touch. And here he was at the Festival. Was he in the business and Howard didn't know about it?

The more they drank the more the history of their lost years came to light.

Danny Ballantyne had become a professional thug, a bona fide bad guy right out of the Scorsese mold. Howard froze a smile on his face, nodding his head up and down as his old high-school chum described segments of his career in detail.

Danny had a young lady with him who hailed from California. He introduced her telling Howard that he was her bodyguard. She was a knockout. Howard was impressed. Although only in her twenties she had worldly class. Howard focused on her to keep the panic away from hearing about Danny's exploits.

Who knows? She may be a star on the horizon. She had looks and could talk without mumbling, a real advantage in this business. At least concentrating on her was keeping Howard calm.

Solomon was one of the judges at the festival and in his jovial mood he drank a little too much and began to focus even more on Danny's client. Ballantyne took no notice.

Somehow their conversation turned from classic films to museum artworks and the lost collections of prominent Jewish families during the war. This was a subject Howard was more than familiar with. The Solomon family collection had been confiscated in Poland after the invasion. Howard's grandfather had lost his life in the process.

Howard was being sucked in. This little shiksa was intelligent to boot! As they continued to talk she told him about a man in California who had a huge collection of art confiscated by the Nazis that he had smuggled into the states after the war. This ravishing youngster got Howard so worked up in his alcoholic state that he was ready to fly back home and deal with the situation personally; just like in the movies. "Ah…there's the rub."

Just like in the movies.

In his lifetime spent creating cinematic fantasies Howard had nourished the bad habit of confusing make-believe with reality. A team of psychologists had treated him for this condition for years. Howard never seemed to be clear in his life; never sure of his place. To him, he lived in the imagination. There was the French nation, the German nation, the Spanish nation but for Howard there was only the imagination.

That night in Utah, in a slushy-drunken-stupor-mindset he pictured himself a potential hero. He was the big-shot of the group. He had the connections. He was with his old high school buddy who was probably on the FBI's most wanted list. Hell, he could just reach across the table to Danny and plan a hit on the SOB in Pasadena with the stolen art, right here in the bar and be done with it. Justice would be served.

The twenty-something cutie had suggested kidnapping the old man's granddaughter. Danny liked that idea and he said he could put it in motion with a couple of phone calls.

Howard dove right into the pond, head first.

They clinked their glasses and Howard yelled "Let's do it!" at the top of his lungs completely out of his mind from too much booze and a little coke.

This outburst drew the curiosity of several journalists sitting nearby.

Danny called him at his hotel the next day and asked for the contact number of an independent film crew which would shoot anywhere in the world for a fee. Howard coughed up a couple of potentials and then forgot that evening until months later when he read about the kidnapping online and knew that it must be Danny, possibly spurred on by that little chick he had with him in Utah.

In a panic he made another crucial mistake. He called a private security company he had used before when he was being stalked by an obsessive fan to have them to find out if anyone outside of official law enforcement was working the case. They got back to him with a name. Arnold Blackburn. Howard authorized the agency to have a one-on-one with the P.I. to convince him to drop his role in the investigation. When the agency reported back the Academy Award winner found out they'd gone a bit too far. Howard Solomon was sinking deeper into the quicksand. Once again, reality and fantasy were at loggerheads in his brain.

"What in the hell was I thinking?"

Howard had been a member of ARCA since its inception and he knew that the society was working 24/7 to get artwork confiscated during the war returned to the proper owners. Some members of the community such as Abe Meyers already had word from reliable sources that precious paintings were on their way home.

On top of this career crisis in the middle of Tunisia, the actual kidnapping that he had co-conceived was now completely out of control back Stateside.

If the authorities ever caught on that he was behind this insane scheme he'd be watching movies on a black and white TV from Folsom instead of making them.

Howard couldn't believe he'd been such an idiot. His sweaty palm could barely grasp his cell phone. He punched the number over and over to no avail. His old high school chum was not picking up. Howard cut the power to his cell and slipped it into his pocket.

His brother Marvin had become a jeweler. Why hadn't he thought of that?

Twenty

FBI Special Agent Chris Clarke stared out beneath the rim of his San Diego Padres baseball cap at the love of his life. The weather around his South Mission Beach condo was crisp and the fall shoreline gray except for patches of sun that occasionally peeked through the clouds: typical for November. The murky sky increased his feelings of guilt. He knew he had neglected her— she looked twice her age.

It was truly criminal. How long had they been together? He recalled the day they met—love at first sight. She went home with him right there and then and they've been together ever since. He knew that it was around ten years ago but sadly, he wasn't sure. She stood in silence. They had been so content over the years but now that didn't seem to matter. He approached her and stroked her but she didn't respond. A sharp pain shot through him. She deserved better.

Well, here we go.

Armed with a two gallon bucket full of soapy water and an industrial strength sponge, he set out to make things right. He showered his 1971 Porsche 911e Targa, performing an ablution. He managed one swipe with the sponge across the car's top and his cell phone went off. He cursed beneath his breath then checked the caller ID.

It was Carlos 'Chubbs' Gonzales, his partner who had saved his life as well as many others on their last case. Chubbs was more to him than a partner, more like a glove that fit perfectly.

"Wha's up Chief?"

Chris continued with the hose. "I was just giving Suzie a bath."

"Who in the hell is Suzie?"

"What do you mean by that? Christ, you see her every day."

No response.

"…My Porsche, you moron!"

Chubbs laughed. "Well you may have to postpone that erotic event. I just got a text from Chief Gerrard. We're due to arrive in the city of angels and assholes by late afternoon today. They need us on the Fick kidnapping pronto."

"…Anything new?"

Chubb's sounded grave. "This puppy isn't following the pattern. No ransom note yet and one of L.A.'s finest took a bullet two nights ago while tailing a possible suspect. Chief of Police McCrary was informed that the grandfather of the victim received a communication from what can now be officially called the kidnappers. We're up partner."

"What's the status of the shot cop?"

"…Too soon to know but hopes are high."

Chris looked at Suzie dripping wet. "Pick me up in an hour unless you'd care to come over now and offer me a hand giving a mature woman a bath and a rub down?"

Chubbs chuckled and closed his cell.

Chris turned off the hose and put Suzie in the garage dripping wet. He went inside to pack which never took very long. He always had a bag half-ready to go. Part of the job description.

A few moments later Chubbs pulled into the driveway and beeped his horn. Chris grabbed his gear, eye-checked the condo and headed out the door. His partner was holding up two Styrofoam coffee cups brandishing his Cheshire-cat smile.

Gotta love this guy.

Twenty-one

Chief Mac was in his office when the call came in. Arney updated him, telling him about his interview with the mystery woman in Venice.

McCreary asked him to be in his office in an hour. There were new developments since this morning.

"Will this be accompanied by a light, early evening snack?" Arney jabbed at the police chief.

"No, on the contrary, you might be dining late. Two Special FBI Agents from San Diego are on their way here now. I told them about your involvement and of course they want to talk. I'm not so sure they're that happy with my decision to call in someone off the grid." The police chief took a breath. "At any rate, I need you here by seven o'clock. We clear?"

Arney was glad that McCreary couldn't see the expression on his face. Just what I need, he thought, the FBI up my ass for a look-see. He forced a smile. "Whatever you say Mac, I'll see you at seven."

The P.I. hung up the phone and stood there for a minute. He wandered into the kitchen looking for a cookie and spotted the keys which Victor had given him. He sat by his front window and called locksmiths in the Long Beach area.

On the fifth number he hit a winner. The owner, Joseph Lobo, had a record of those serial numbers and the customer's name. Arney wrote down the name. "....Wilbur Smith, uh huh..." Definitely a phony. "Tell me Mr. Lobo, could you describe the man to me?"

Joseph Lobo laughed as he told him that he'd been blind since birth.

Arney thanked the locksmith for his time and hung up wondering how in the hell do you grind a key if you can't see? It didn't matter. Lobo had given him the date of purchase which was about two weeks before the kidnapping: plenty of time to put together a stash-house for the victim.

He heated up two pieces of leftover pizza and ate them on the way downtown. He would need something on his stomach to deal with two of the FBI's finest for the rest of the evening. The interview would probably be a waste of time for all of those involved. He took the keys with him just in case he decided to really come clean.

Arney could hear voices coming from Mac's office. He knocked on the door. "Am I late?"

Mac rose from his desk. Special Agents Clarke and Gonzales stood up.

When Chubbs and Arney made eye contact they gasped. "You're shittin' me, is that you, Gonzales?"

Chubbs was already moving toward Arney with his arms extended wearing his Cheshire-cat grin. 'Blackburn, you son a bitch, where in the hell did you come from?" The two men embraced and started to laugh. Chubbs at six feet four inches looked like he was hugging a stuffed toy.

"Sorry," Chubbs said as they let each other go. He looked at his boss. "Chris Clarke, meet Arnold Blackburn, the fastest tight end the UCLA Bruins ever had in their lineup."

Chris shook hands with Arney and the two men smiled at each other. Chubbs explained that while attending UCLA they both played varsity football. Arnold was offense and the big fellow defense. They played the Rose Bowl before graduating.

Chubbs spoke. "Hell man, I didn't know that you were on the force. When did all of this happen?" Arney looked a bit embarrassed and Chief Mac took over.

"Sit down gentlemen." Mac addressed Chris and Chubbs. "Arnold was a lieutenant on the LAPD until an unfortunate incident got him kicked off the force. I issued him a private detective's license because I felt that Internal affairs had gone too far." Mac looked over at Arney. "Blackburn was a damn good cop and now he's in the private sector. I asked him to come on board because of his unofficial street connections and his savvy with the criminal sector of our community."

McCreary returned his attention to Chris and Chubbs. "This Fick kidnapping has got the mayor in an uproar. Honestly, between the LAPD and your people at the Bureau, we've got very little to show for our efforts. As you are probably aware, the kidnapping took place last week and so far there hasn't been a ransom note, but Arney has been able to uncover more facts than anyone so far, so here we are."

Arney looked at Chubbs.

Seeing his old friend had changed the atmosphere considerably. It also changed Arney's attitude toward the Feds.

Twenty-two

Chris and Chubbs checked into their hotel tired and hungry. They made arrangements with Arney to meet downstairs in a half an hour for dinner. Afterwards they'd talk.

By ten o'clock room service had brought a carafe of coffee up to Chris's suite and they settled down to business. Throughout dinner, Chris observed Chubbs and Arney as they caught up on their lives since UCLA and reminisced about their time on campus.

One matter dogged Chris while they dined. As long as Blackburn was one of the good guys he might be useful to the team as a consultant. But, if somehow he became a suspect then there would be a definite conflict of interest and Chubbs would be off the case.

The rule was standard across the board: any law enforcement investigator assigned to a case cannot have known the suspect prior to their involvement. If so, then they are obligated to remove themselves from the investigation. No exceptions.

Chris poured coffee as the lights of downtown L.A. shimmered along the windows of the seventeenth floor. Chris took a sip and looked at Arney. "So, Blackburn, how in the hell did you get booted off the force?

Mac treats you like one of his own and I know you don't make lieutenant by directing traffic. What gives?"

Arney stretched his legs out and yawned. "To tell you truth Clarke, it was a case of wrong place, wrong time. Undercover was doing a sting on the Bigelow Brothers. Ever heard of them?"

Chris and Chubbs shook their heads in the negative.

"Well, they're about the most powerful pimps in California. They've got houses and call-girls in every municipality. One of the undercover team was sick the night they decided to do a bust and they asked me to sub. It was reported that about a dozen of their high-end delicacies were working out of a West Hollywood hotel. I was to present myself as a client and I took that responsibility seriously."

Chubbs laughed. Chris didn't.

"When the bust came down a rookie started to beat the crap out of the hooker I was with. I snapped. I gave him a pretty good pounding. A little more than I'd planned on, but in the heat of the moment...." Arney gazed out the window. "Anyway, Internal Affairs immediately kicked my ass out the door. Chief Mac called me the next day and we talked. He rushed the paperwork through for my P.I. license and here we are. Welcome to L.A. boys."

The three men toasted each other, cups in the air, then Chubbs queried.

"So, the Chief pulled you in on the kidnapping, in the hopes that you might get some leads from the other side of the fence?"

Arney poured all another cup. "You've got it right down to the wording. Mac thought my street connections might have info that the uniforms and suits wouldn't be privy to. So far, on this case, it's been paying off."

Arney paused to think about his next move. "You guys crossed paths with Victor Gastaldi yet?"

Chubbs jumped in. "He's on our list of 'to do' things. His loan sharking and narcotics activities are starting to build quite a reputation at the Bureau."

Blackburn smiled as he began to tell Chris and Chubbs the story of his being abducted by one of Victor's goons and his talk that afternoon with Victor at his well-protected estate downtown.

"Victor is a strange one. He's well organized and always seems to be one jump ahead of the police. He's never been officially busted. They haul him in for questioning from time to time but after an hour of two he heads back home. I'm sure he's got one or two of LAPD's finest on his payroll. There can't be another answer."

Chris was re-energized. "So why did Gastaldi invite you over?"

"At first he wanted to hire me to follow a Chicago bad guy who had recently arrived in L.A. Victor heard rumors that this gangster wanted in on his action." Arney laughed. "There I was in big-time dope dealer Gastaldi's front room being offered a job to keep tabs on another crook. I couldn't believe it. Then, something strange happened. When I told him that I wasn't interested in the job, he brought up the Fick disappearance and hinted that this guy from Chicago, Danny Ballantyne may be involved. My interest picked up. When I left I had an envelope with his photos, a business card with Victor's private cell number, a check made out for way too much money and also, two keys."

Chubbs reacted. "Two keys…? What's that all about?"

Arney rubbed his eyes. "That's what I asked. Victor wanted me to find out what locks they fit. They might be connected to the kidnapping. I spoke with some of my old contacts and found out the keys were sold by a locksmith in Long Beach around six weeks ago. That puts the items in the timeframe of the kidnapping." Arney yawned. "Who the fuck knows— maybe the kidnappers have the girl stashed away somewhere in L.A. county and Victor knows more than he's letting on?"

Chris glanced at his watch. It was one in the morning. "Let's wrap it up for now and get some rest." Chris turned to Arney as they all stood. "I'd like to pick this conversation up tomorrow." Chris opened up his wallet and took out a card. "Call me at this number when you're up and running."

Arney shook hands with Chris and gave Chubbs a big hug.

The drive back to Silver Lake from downtown would only take ten minutes. The exhausted detective hoped he could put together a plan before he walked through his front door. Time was flying by and his mind was running on fumes. He hoped he'd put the milk back in the fridge.

He needed a cookie.

Twenty-three

Inside the decaying mansion it was cold. Victor Gastaldi closed his cell phone and shivered. He stared out the bay window watching the shadows of his night-time security lighting which created an eerie glow as they reflected off tall weeds weaving in the wind.

His sister hadn't been in touch with him for almost a year. She had just paid him a visit and told him that she was gay. Oddly enough, even though he was raised in a dysfunctional family, Victor was strongly Catholic and his anti-gay feelings ran deep inside him. He was a prominent drug lord who used strong arm tactics when necessary to make a point with a client. But, Dee was family. He could never wish her any harm no matter what she did.

His memories of their childhood were not pleasant with his father in jail most of the time and his mother whoring to keep the household together. Dee Dee was three years older than Victor but he'd always felt like her big brother. As they grew up, he took the responsibility of protecting her.

He wondered if Arney had found out anything about the two keys that Dee had left behind the day she came to make amends; the day she came out of the closet. As Victor listened to her confession he exploded and nearly destroyed an entire room. Victor's temper was legendary and when it went off it was better to be somewhere else.

Today he had more of a problem than Dee's sexual preference. In her hasty attempt to get back in his good graces she had confessed to her brother that she had gone to the Hilton Hotel on Sunset and shot a policeman thinking it was the Chicago gangster.

The nervous king of drug trafficking and loan sharking lit a cigarette and stuffed it into his ivory holder. He was alone in his castle, pacing around from room to room: First upstairs, then downstairs. He wasn't sure what to do.

In a curious way he was proud of Dee for her attempt to remove a new enemy from Victor's turf, but he knew that the police didn't wear badges and uniforms for nothing. They would eventually figure out who did it. After all, it was one of their own who got shot and that meant that no one in the department would rest until the shooter was brought in.

He was mulling over several plans in his head to get Dee out of the area to start a new life somewhere far away from here.

Victor headed outside towards the swimming pool. He looked up and actually saw stars, a rare occurrence in the night-lit sky in the L.A. basin. The water in the pool was full of leaves and murky. It was so dark he didn't see the reflection of the figure approaching him from behind until it was too late.

Twenty-four

For the first time in a week Arney slept through the entire night. He woke up to the sound of gulls cawing as they circled the lake looking for their morning meal. He had just put the boiling water into his French press when the phone rang. It was Chief Mac.

Arney pressed down on the coffee maker. "Top of the morning to you Chief, how's our day looking so far?"

Mac answered in a cold voice. "Turn on your TV to channel 2."

Arney poured a quick half cup of coffee and flipped on the tube. He recognized the house as Victor Gastaldi's. He sat down. The journalist on the scene was describing the event that had taken place there.

"Well known L.A. gangster Victor Gastaldi was found dead, early this morning, shot in the head beside the swimming pool at his MacArthur Park estate. Preliminary reports indicate that the murder might have gangland connections.

He was discovered next to his swimming pool by one of his body guards who always reported to his boss in the morning. The coroner states that death was instantaneous and that the shooting probably occurred sometime after midnight. Spokesperson for the LAPD has told this reporter that Victor Gastaldi's death will be treated like any other murder investigation that the

83

department handles. This is Maxine Hermann, channel 2 morning news, live from MacArthur Park. Back to you Bill…

Arney grabbed the phone. "What the fuck Mac, what's going on?"

McCreary sounded out of breath. "That's what we'd all like to know." He paused for a moment. "After your talk with the Feds last night did you go directly home?"

Arney's temper blew. "Fuck you. How could you think for even one minute that I would do something like this? I certainly didn't like the rat-bastard but I wouldn't off him, not now. He was an important link in the chain. I was planning on talking to him after I found out more about those keys he gave me. You son-of-a-bitch!"

McCreary shouted. 'Now calm down Arney, I didn't think you had anything to do with it, but I had to ask, to eliminate you from the picture. By your own admission you were with the victim this week. It's just procedure, you know that. Give me a break."

Arney's coffee was getting cold. "Fuck you and fuck procedure!" He slammed the phone down and ran outside to stand next to the chain-link fence of the lake. He fished into his pocket and found the card from Chris Clarke. He dialed the number and waited wondering if he had made a mistake letting the mystery woman of Venice out of his net.

Chris answered his cell sounding distracted. "Hey Chris, it's Arney. Did you hear the news?"

Chris was shuffling paper. "Nope, haven't had a chance; trying to get everything ready for our setup at City Hall this morning."

"Victor Gastaldi was murdered last night shortly after we broke up our talk." Arney waited for Clarke to react.

"Who told you?"

"Chief Mac called me just before I called you. He wanted to know if I had anything to do with it…"

Chris shot back—"Did you?"

Arney was boiling again. "Well may I offer you the same salutation I put forth to the Chief of the Los Angeles' Police Department?"

Chris chuckled, he knew what was coming.

"Fuck you and kiss my ass!

Chris moved past the moment. "Listen Arney, this is really important. Some party or person offs Victor Gastaldi shortly after he hires you to shadow another bad guy who Victor thinks, or knows, is involved with the kidnapping. There's a connection here that we're not making." Chris paused for a moment to see if he could feel Arney on the other end of the line. "You still there?"

"I'm with you, go…"

"Tell me Blackburn, who's at the top of your list to take care of Gastaldi for good and why now?"

Arney had moved into the kitchen to get a refill of French Roast. "My instincts tell me that it is not another gangster; this one feels way off the chart. Nope, I think that his murder was planned for a long time by someone off our grid, and the opportunity arrived and they jumped on it. I don't feel a connection to organized crime or the kidnapping. This one feels personal." Arney bit into a cookie. "My money is on a crime of passion. I wish to hell I could tell you who or why? But I haven't got shit to back up my theory. Sometimes a chill comes over me when I'm getting close. It has nothing to do with facts, just my imagination coming up with a possibility which offers no guarantees. Sorry bud, but that's it."

Chris was surprised to find another lawman who, like himself, received chills around his neck and shoulders when his mind was led down a certain path, no matter how ridiculous the theory appears at first sight. "Tell me Arney, did you read Sherlock Holmes as a kid?"

Arney laughed. "What do you mean did I…?

They both laughed. They busted each other. They were still reading Conan Doyle.

Twenty-five

Chris and Chubbs were installed one floor below the Mayor's office.

Arney arrived sharp at two o'clock.

"Nice digs the Mayor coughed up for you guys. Cozy and convenient. His highness is just a floor away."

Chubbs smiled, Chris didn't.

The P.I. could tell that Clarke was all business today. Here's a guy who will be on a different planet every day. That's okay. Arney knew that his challenge would be to tame his smart-ass attitude. He wished himself luck: a futile gesture.

Chris cut to the quick. "Do you have any more ideas about who may have taken out Gastaldi?"

"I've been mulling that over since we talked this morning. Honestly, not even a definite maybe."

Chubbs asked, "Okay then tell me, what's with this kidnapping? Why do it if you're not asking for cash?"

Arney sat down in the only other chair in the office. "Because this kidnapping is more complex than the powers-that-be think it is. I believe that Victor had a direct link to the crime through his sister, Dee Dee."

Arney flicked open his phone to the picture of Gail Goodman he'd taken at the Venice café. Chubbs took the phone and plugged in an adapter so that the picture would come up on their laptop.

Chris looked at Arney. "Tell us about her."

"The ladies name is Gail Goodman. She claims to be the lesbian lover of Gastaldi's sister. She also believes that Dee Dee is involved in the kidnapping."

Chubbs was taking notes. "Did you know that Victor had a sister when you interviewed her?"

"Didn't have a clue."

Chris jumped in. "What did this Gail Goodman tell you about Gastaldi's sister being involved?"

Arney recounted the conversation he had with her at the Venice Café.

Chris looked down at the floor. "Does this put us any closer to a solution?"

Arney put his hands behind his head. "Well, for one thing we may have someone who is actually on the scene, maybe even a watchdog at the stash house. They kidnapped a woman so, logical to have a woman guarding her even if she is a lesbian." Arney smiled. "Maybe even a better reason."

Arney reached into his pocket and pulled out the two keys Victor had given him. He tossed them on the table. "I think that Dee Dee visited her brother recently and left these keys behind. They could be a spare pair that unlocks the doors where our victim is being held. He was very insistent about knowing what locks these keys belonged to.

"I got lucky and was able to trace them down. They were sold in Long Beach about six weeks ago. That would fit in with our timeline for the kidnapping. My guess is she is being held somewhere in the area where these keys were sold."

Chris took out a cigarette and lit it. Smoking was banned in all County buildings. "You know something Blackburn? I think that you've just about got this case wrapped up."

Arney looked around their new office space hoping a pot of coffee would magically appear.

The exhausted P.I. stood up and stretched. "Yeah, I've got some things scoped out but this shit is much deeper than the kidnapping. I mean the person or persons that thought this up are not criminal types." Arney looked over at Chris. "You ever heard of ARCA?"

Chris stubbed out his cigarette. "ARCA is linked to our new Art Crimes division at the Bureau." He locked eyes with Arney. "Are you telling me that Fick is a possible ARCA target? Is that the reason there hasn't been a ransom note? A million or so in change wouldn't be enough?"

The sun had moved to the other side of the county building. The room suddenly turned three shades darker.

Arney's voice came from the shadows. "Boys, I think there is *trouble in River City*, if you know what I mean."

Twenty-six

Arney headed home to get it together. He was just about to take a bite of his tuna sandwich when someone knocked on the front door. He crept up to the bay window and saw the shapely rear end of Conchita Morales on the porch. She bolted in as if someone were chasing her. Arney cautiously looked outside in both directions, saw no one.

The twenty-something Latina had been crying her eyes out. Her face was a mess. Mascara running in all directions and her eyes puffed up like balloons. Arney realized for the first time that Conchita was attractive. Even with her stressed-out presence, she had a real warmth and glow about her. He pulled himself back to reality.

"Okay, what's going on? Why are you here?"

She reached across the dining table for a Kleenex and blew her nose and wiped her eyes. "I didn't know where to go. After I heard about Victor I..." She broke down into tears and Arney let her ride it on out. "I didn't know what to do. The Bigelow brothers are trying to find me and I thought about how nice you were the other day so I came here. I don't really know why." She looked into his eyes with that all too familiar plea for help. "I don't want to go back to that life again. Not ever!"

Arney offered her the other half of his sandwich. She waved him off then a few seconds later took a bite. He watched her cowering figure eat in silence and he tried to think what would be the best thing to do. He had noticed the day she returned his gun from Victor's house, that not only did he find her interesting but his emotional canvas, blank for a long time, was now beginning to display blotches of color. Just what he needed: attracted to a Latina hooker half his age. Time to get it together.

'Okay. Listen, I have to go out for a couple of hours. I need you to stay here and keep out of sight. The police will have some questions for you regarding Victor and you'll be much better off in my care than running around on the streets. Do you think anyone followed you here?"

Conchita shyly shook her head. "I don't know. I wasn't paying attention. I just drove in a fog."

Clouds were gathering over the lake. He stood at his bay window taking it in for a few moments to clear his mind. Even though Conchita Morales was a hooker, somehow for reasons unknown, he thought he could trust her. She was scared and alone. Arney had always been a sucker for a damsel in distress. He sat down next to Conchita taking her hands in his.

"Listen to me. Do not under any circumstances think about going anywhere and do not open the door no matter what." Arney rifled through her purse and took out her car keys. He put them in his pocket. He winked at her. "Just a little insurance."

He showed her the spare bedroom in the back of his house and said he would be back in a few hours. He would return with dinner. She laughed when he told her that if she got hungry there was a fresh batch of chocolate chip cookies in the kitchen.

Arney kissed her on the forehead and headed out making sure that she locked the door behind him. He sat in his car for a few minutes just down the block to see if anyone was going to approach his house after he left. Everything looked good.

The confused and conflicted private-eye drove down Silver Lake Boulevard heading toward MacArthur Park wondering just what the fuck he was getting himself into?

Twenty-seven

When Arney arrived at Victor's Chris and Chubbs were already at it. The tension in the atmosphere between the LAPD and the two FBI Special Agents was tenable. Arney wasn't so sure that his presence might not cause a little more stress being that many of his ex-colleagues were on the scene.

He found the pair out by the swimming pool talking with the M.E. Chris asked, "So, you don't think that the victim lived long after the bullet entered his brain?"

The Medical Examiner, a typically fatigued looking man, past middle-age replied with an automatic-pilot monotone. "My opinion: death was instantaneous. There was no prolonged agony. No torture. I'm thinking contract kill. Forensics hasn't come up with one shred of evidence around the pool. No footprints, fibers, fingerprints or foreign DNA. This person was a pro, no two ways about it." He looked up at Chris and Chubbs with a smile. "...And if they weren't, they sure got lucky."

The city's death collector packed up his gear. He looked at the three men. "Of course, my opinions are not based on fact, just thirty years of experience and a hunch now and then that turns out to be correct. I leave this mess in your capable hands gentlemen." Their eyes followed him in silence as he trundled away.

Chris to Arney. "Who's in charge here as far as you can guess?"

"Probably Detective Donald Jacobson. I saw him in the house when I arrived passing out orders to the crew."

Chris lit another cigarette. "Let's find him. We need to go through every piece of evidence."

Donald Jacobson was fine with the two FBI Agents but he had an unsure look when he spied the ex-cop.

Chris noticed. "He's with us...officially."

Arney to Jacobson: "You guys picked up Bernie Needlebaum or any of Gastaldi's other henchmen?"

The Leary detective replied, "Yeah, we caught the big 'B' as he was arriving this morning to check in with Victor. The two on-sight bodyguards are also cooling their heels downtown. APB's are out on the rest of the crew." Feeling that he had doled out enough info for the moment, Jacobson excused himself.

The trio headed for Victor's office, the old library of the mansion. The drawers of his desk had been emptied and all of their contents placed in plastic bags and tagged.

One of the LAPD forensic personnel was at a table going through Victor's computer. Chris walked over to her and introduced himself. He told the woman that he would need to know what she found in his files and Chris gave her his card. She went back to the screen.

Chubbs was sorting through the plastic bags on the desk. Arney decided to wander around the room letting whatever caught his eye take precedent. There a series of photographs pinned to a cork-board panel behind the desk. Most of the photos were bent from the humidity except for one which looked fairly new. It was a picture of Victor with his arm around a woman near his age. Both were smiling into the camera as if they meant it. Her features had a masculine tinge. Arney figured that she might be Victor's sister, Dee Dee.

"Hey Chubbs, get a load of this."

"Who do you think that is?" By now Chris had joined them.

Arney tapped the picture. "My guess is that this is Victor's sister Dee Dee, who my contact in Venice suspects that she is in on the kidnapping."

Chris took the picture and stared at it a few moments and Chubbs bagged it. He looked at Arney. "McCreary tells me that you tailed Fick to his rendezvous in Griffith Park and that the old man left with a small package that was hidden behind his bench, that right?"

Arney's thoughts were on Conchita, hoping she was safe. "Yep, and when I went to his house at three in the morning for a surprise visit I mentioned it and he clammed up. Whatever was in that package is probably more important than we can imagine."

Chris and Chubbs were due at Fick's residence within the hour.

Arney chuckled. "Make sure you have a full tank. From the entrance of his property to his front door takes about two minutes at ten miles per hour."

The LAPD had found a good deal of substances, firearms and cash on the property, but nothing unusual. As Arney walked through the weeds towards the front gate he turned back for one last look at Zanzibar.

That same afternoon Victor Gastaldi's former right-hand-man Bernie Needlebaum was in a holding cell downtown. The cramped room was crowded with the District Attorney and his assistant as well as a Court appointed Attorney assigned to the gangster. All the legal mouths were moving fast in heated argument over Bernie's future. The big "B" wasn't paying much attention. Victor's Beverly Hills mouthpiece was still on retainer and would show up soon and then it would be time to listen. Bernie wasn't what one could describe as smart, but he had smarts.

In their long association over the years Victor had divulged all of his business dealings to Bernie and made him privy to the hidden accounts of those persons on the inside of the law who secretly took payoffs to keep Gastaldi's machine running smoothly. Bernie knew their names and where the actual files were kept which implicated these cops and politicians in Victor's rackets, along with the exact amounts which had been paid out. The police were crawling all over the estate but that didn't bother Bernie. The files were hidden in plain sight. The cops would never find them.

Except for his being a known collaborator with a faction of the criminal element in the city of angels, there was nothing that law enforcement could pin on him specifically. In the course of his career he had been arrested twice and released on bail pending charges. Said charges were mysteriously absent when the time came to submit them.

Everyone knew by now that he had "escorted" Arnold Blackburn to Gastaldi's mansion for an impromptu meeting, but if the ex LAPD Detective didn't press charges there was nothing which could be made out of it. Bernie didn't think that he would.

While the three attorneys were conducting a heated debate as to Needlebaum's future, the former right-hand man for one of L.A.'s top drug and extortion moguls was quietly hatching his own plans and contemplating the cash that it should generate. Bernie was feeling a new confidence he had never felt before.

The King is dead—long-live the king.

Twenty-eight

There were no lights on in his house when Arney returned. Everything was quiet. He opened the front door slowly. "Hey babe, it's me, are you okay?" Not a sound. He set down the bag of groceries, pulled out his 9 mil Colt and tip-toed down the hallway to the spare bedroom. Sweat was forming on his brow. He feared the worst. He slowly preened open the door to find Conchita fast asleep, snoring slightly. She was under the covers and her clothes were strewn about the room.

He headed for the kitchen. He grabbed a bottle of milk from the fridge and took a cookie from the plate. This had been one hell of a week.

Arney knew that Chris and Chubbs would be on his case for harboring a prime witness in Gastaldi's murder, but he was thinking that he'd have a better chance of getting some useful information if he talked to her first. Conchita appeared to trust him right now and that was a plus.

Arney mused on the fact that the cast of this real-life melodrama was highlighted by two abused women: the kidnapped granddaughter of a billionaire and a Latina prostitute; both around the same age whose lives couldn't be further apart.

It had been a nearly a week since Chief McCrary called him in on this case. So much had happened in that amount of time that Arney's head was spinning. Gary Bub nearly whacked— Gastaldi murdered.

As he bit into cookie number two, he wondered if he was really capable of handling Conchita for a night. Would he be able to keep his hands off of her? The thought gave him a lump in his throat. He unpacked the groceries and began to fix dinner for the two of them.

Yes, this had been a hell of a week!

Twenty-nine

Chris unbuckled his seatbelt at the Fick gate and leaned over into the speakerphone to announce their arrival. True to Arney's word, it took a minute or so to arrive at the front door.

Chubbs mouth was agape. "Jesus Christ, how in the hell can anyone afford to do this? This place is a hotel!"

Chris got his attention. "I think it's going to be good cop, bad cop time. You take the sweetheart role, I'll be the asshole."

Chubbs grinned. "Type casting works for me." Chris smiled.

Before the two agents could ring a bell the door was opened by a butler who instructed them to wait in the library while he fetched the owner. The room was dark and had a strange vibe about it. It felt sad.

"Good evening gentlemen, I'm Ezekiel Fick, and you must be...?"

Chris and Chubbs showed their ID's as they introduced themselves. Ezekiel Fick was about to offer tea or coffee when Chris cut him off. "This isn't a social call Mr. Fick. You need to tell us right now, every bit of information that you have concerning your granddaughter's disappearance and that includes what was in the package you picked up at Griffith Park."

The immediate aggressiveness shocked Fick. "I'm not accustomed to taking orders. The President of the United States consults with me weekly!"

Bad cop Chris shot back. "I don't give a shit if you're giving Putin a shiatsu massage and a blow job. You've got the world turned upside down to find your granddaughter and you're not being straight with those that are busting their ass to find her." Chris's ears were turning red. "I've got half a mind to arrest you right now for withholding evidence." Chris took out a cigarette and lit it without checking to see if there was an ashtray anywhere. "If you'd like, we can make this official and go downtown where we can spend the rest of the night in a room considerably smaller than this one."

Good cop Chubbs took over. "Whoa partner, I'm sure that Mr. Fick is more than anxious to have his granddaughter returned safely." Both agents stared at Fick. "Isn't that right sir?"

The old man lost it. He swayed on his feet and fell in a seated position on one of the leather couches. Tears were rolling down his cheeks. He waved his arm towards two chairs. Chris and Chubbs sat through Fick's emotional ride. "I don't know what the hell to do any more. Stephanie is my entire life. If anything has happened to her, if she has been sexually abused or worse..." Another gush of tears took over.

Chris waited until he seemed to be calming down and then plunged right in. "We're doing our best to find Stephanie but we need all the help we can get from persons like you who are holding back evidence. What was in the package you picked up at Griffith Park and where is it?"

Fick pulled a handkerchief out of his jacket pocket and blew his nose. He went over to his desk for his laptop. "This is what the kidnappers left for me at the park." Fick pushed a key and the video started. Chris and Chubbs were totally focused on the few minutes that it took to run. The final shot was the question frozen on the screen for five seconds. --"*Do You Remember?*'

The screen went to black and Chris turned to Ezekiel Fick. "So, do you?"

Fick slumped as though defeated. "I do. But whoever has kidnapped my granddaughter has made one hell of a mistake."

Chubbs pulled his chair around to face Fick on the couch. 'Well then sir now's the time to let it all hang out." He placed a digital recorder on the coffee table and the reluctant billionaire began.

The duo exited the Fick estate and headed towards Orange Grove Boulevard. Chubbs drove. "Hey partner, do you think the old man's being square with us?"

Chris lit a cigarette and blew out the smoke slowly. "I think what I've thought after all interviews; that a witness or suspect is telling some, but not all of the truth. Everyone holds back something.

"My curiosity is extremely peaked by what he claims his uncle left him. I had read the story by Ambroise Vollard when I was getting my art degree. Fick's uncle was very smart. Ezekiel could never be held accountable for art works which technically don't exist. The partially damaged Monet canvases which Roderich Fick left for his nephew at the end of the war are really mythic, rumored to be floating around for decades. They've never been seen or catalogued. There's no record." Chris flicked an ash. "They would be valuable even in their mutilated condition, but worth many millions if they had been restored by a world-class expert. Historically they would be priceless in today's market."

Chris rubbed his eyes. "What did you notice about the video?"

Chubbs was stopped at a crosswalk. "It looked professional to me. Not something a kidnapper would do on an Iphone or a hand-held video camera."

Chris tossed his cigarette out. "Exactly. It had commercial quality, as if one of Hollywood's finest were behind the camera."

Chubbs braked for pedestrians. "You're shittin' me, you don't think that some of the film industry folks within ARCA are out for Fick's blood? That's insane."

Chris needed a pack of smokes keeping an eye out for a 7/11. "You know how I work bud. Something grabs me a certain way and I start to see things. That kidnapper's video was HD and edited by a pro. Nothing ragged about the camera sweeps." Chris spotted a store about two blocks away. He pointed it out to Chubbs. "Remember when I went to Europe a few years back to help recover that statue stolen from a private collection in Paris?"

Chubbs nodded as he pulled up into the 7/11 parking lot.

Chris patted his coat for his wallet. "While I was there the collector was ragging on the local gendarmes for not having tried hard enough to recover the artwork stolen from his parents by the Nazis. It seems that there's more stolen collections floating around than was previously thought. And what's even scarier is the possibility that powerful persons who are not in law enforcement are tired of waiting around for things to happen." Chris stared out of the window and sighed. "They could be taking matters in their own hands. In this case they're way off target. If Fick is telling the truth about the total stash his uncle left him, none of these paintings were ever in any collection."

Chris gave Chubbs a serious look. "If it's possible that the kidnapping was planned by people in the film industry, they're having a hard time separating reality from fiction." Chris got out and leaned into the car. "And as we continue to chase the bad guys, my good friend and partner, it makes the bad guys much harder to nail, because they appear to be good guys; good guys with big-time clout!"

Chris returned with a carton of smokes. As he fastened his seatbelt Chubbs spoke, "I was just thinking that the old man sure has a lot of interesting art work on his walls. Should we send in the Bureau experts to see if any of it is part of the Nazi loot that ARCA is hunting for?"

"I don't think we'll find anything on the ARCA list in his house. We need to determine whether or not he's come clean about the total his uncle left him."

Chris turned to Chubbs. "Did you see the look on his face when I asked him if he had any treasures left?"

Chubbs took the Pasadena freeway heading downtown. "10-4 chief, I caught that one. His face tightened up when he said that it was all disposed of years ago."

Chris leaned his head back and closed his eyes. "If there were a dozen or so torn canvases he may have disposed of all of them by now. More than likely, most of them are in private collections in Asia or Western Europe...maybe one or two here in the States."

Chubbs was holding back a question he needed to ask and get it over with. "What do you think about Arney, Chief? Do you think he's been straight with us so far?"

Chris looked over at Chubbs and smiled. "You know me partner. I think everyone holds something back until you lay it at their feet."

Thirty

Arney did himself a favor and didn't light any candles for dinner with Conchita. He threw together some pasta and a salad and opened a bottle of wine just to make his cooking more palatable. She had taken a shower and redressed, including applying her makeup that came from a shoulder bag almost as big as she was. When Arney called her to the table he almost fell over. She was stunning. There was no trace of her past upon her face. Her smile was directly connected to some aspect of momentary happiness.

Both were hungry. They ate with purpose and not many words were exchanged. Arney was compiling a list of questions to ask her concerning Victor; what she may have overheard about the kidnapping when she was around him.

For some reason, he wanted to keep her out of the picture altogether. After all, she hasn't got anything to do with the kidnapping or Victor's death…right? That last thought made him cautiously examine its potential.

Jesus, could Conchita have shot Victor last night? It was a good guess that Victor treated her like shit. After all, she was a hooker and was paid to be abused. If he thought like a cop it was definitely possible. She had motive and opportunity. There were plenty of handguns on the property and she more than likely had access to the house at any time.

Arney finished his last bite. "Was that okay?"

The call-girl was still working on her salad. "That's the best meal I've had in weeks."

"Well that's just pathetic. I'm a lousy cook and I know it."

Conchita leaned over toward Arney. "The food is only part of a meal. The company also counts."

She smiled and he melted. This was going to be much harder than he thought. "Well I hate to spoil this moment of culinary delight but I need to ask you a few questions." He pushed himself back from the table. "I'm hoping that your answers will allow me to keep you completely out of the picture."

Conchita was way ahead of him. "Did I kill Victor? No, is the answer. Would I have killed him? …Maybe—maybe not. Victor was a strange man. Sometimes he could be very kind and considerate but most of the time he treated me as the person I am: a whore. In those moments I hated myself more than I hated Victor."

Arney digested her words as she sipped the last drops of wine. Her delivery had been nonchalant as if she were dictating a shopping list.

Conchita rose from the table and began to clear the dishes. For the first time in a long time, Arney was at a loss for words. As a veteran police officer for over twenty years, he had interviewed and in the real meaning of the term, interrogated dozens of criminals. He could sniff out a lie in a minute. There was nothing cheeky about her statement. He believed her. They stood in the kitchen after the dishes were stacked in the sink. 'Did Victor ever mention anything about a kidnapping?" Conchita leaned against the counter with her arms folded beneath her breasts. "I don't think so. Victor didn't say too much to me about his business. I overheard things from time to time when he was doing a drug deal or giving that creep Needlebaum orders. Victor caused a lot of people a good deal of pain. He was sick in that regard." She stared out the kitchen window at the backyard. "He beat the crap out of me twice but that kind of thing just goes with the job."

Arney was quiet. "I think it would be safer for you to spend the night here."

Conchita nodded.

Arney held up a plate of fresh baked Chocolate chip cookies. "…How about some dessert?"

The hooker took two cookies at once. "Got milk?" They laughed.

Arney woke up with a mouth full of hair: Conchita's. He almost started when he realized what had happened. After dinner last night, and a few chocolate-chip cookies, washed down with a half a bottle of Jameson, the inevitable had happened. How could he have let himself into this situation? Simple—he was horny and she was a gorgeous woman who could go the whole nine yards.

The private eye had been around the block more than several times himself, but his night with Conchita set a new standard. He let her sleep and snuck into the kitchen to brew some French press coffee and review the evening.

It started in the front room after the third shot of whisky. She asked Arney if he had cable TV. It made him laugh. "What the hell, you wanna watch "Desperate Housewives?"

Conchita got *that look* on her face. "I was thinking porno."

Arney stared at her full of mixed surprise and anxious expectation. "Honestly, I've never pushed the porno button on the cable box." He was going for the-man-with-the-virgin-eyes concept. "What did you have in mind?"

Conchita quickly made the television ready and doused the lights; all except for a table lamp that cast a pale yellow sheen around the room. She punched the box until a selection of porno movies came up and she entered 'OK' for the movie that she chose and sat back on the couch. She smiled mischievously. "To tell you the truth, it's women together that turns me on."

The film started off with two women meeting in a café and ten minutes later they were in a hotel room hot and heavy into it. Conchita sat on the couch watching intently while sliding her hand down inside her jeans and masturbating. Arney was near cardiac-arrest. At one moment she motioned for him to come near her and she unzipped his pants and sucked him off while he was watching the movie.

That was just the beginning.

They managed to have sex in every room of the house, even in the pantry closet. Conchita knew more tricks than a Vegas magician and Arney had a hard time keeping up. But not keeping *it* up. He had to be out of his fuckin' mind to be doing this.

But the truth of the matter was he really liked her despite her background and who she was. A hooker is a hooker is a hooker, yet Arney knew, or thought he knew, her tender side and it was captivating. She had heart. She had been through an unimaginable hell most of her adult life, but was still in one piece and somehow had maintained her dignity. That's what attracted him to her. She had managed to live a life doling out sex for a living and was still a human being.

Arney had never been around a woman quite like her and it made, for the moment, more sense to be with her than to not.

The love-struck private eye stared out the kitchen window at the garden wondering what other ridiculous rationalities he would come up with. Mid-thought his cell went off. It was Gary Bub—time to head out of the hospital and head for a burger. Arney laughed and told the recovering cop he'd be there within an hour.

Arney went into the bedroom and gave Conchita a peck on the lips. "Stay put my dear I'll be back in a couple of hours." She gave him a sexy salute and he scurried out the front door before his desire got the better of him.

Thirty-one

The two women sat motionless in their car by the side of the road in the Angeles Crest Mountains. A light rain had just begun. It was quiet and peaceful in this less trafficked area. They embraced without moving.

Daryl Jennings, one of three local Highway Patrol officers assigned to the area stopped his squad car about fifty feet behind the parked vehicle. His first thoughts were that they may be having car trouble, but procedure was procedure. He ran the license plate through the onboard computer and it came up on the hot list, belonging to one, Dee Dee Jameson; wanted by LAPD, suspected of shooting a police officer.

Jennings was a veteran of the Patrol and always did things by the book. He called headquarters and told them what he'd found and requested backup. The two figures in the front seat of the car were not moving. In less than two minutes his partner pulled up from the other direction. Jennings jumped on the squawk box and told his back up that he was going to approach the vehicle. He readied his hand gun and walked slowly towards the driver's side. When he got close enough he noticed that the window was down. With an authoritative voice he demanded, "Put your hands on top of your head and don't move."

No response. A bead of sweat trickled down Daryl's shirt. With his gun aimed at the driver he tore open the door. In his twenty years with the patrol Jennings had seen it all, but life as a lawman is full of surprises. Weapon, cocked, he bent down to look inside and almost threw up.

His eyes fell upon two women drenched in blood from separate head wounds still wrapped in each other's arms.

Thirty-two

The In and Out burger joint on Lankershim in North Hollywood was packed with teenagers just out from school. A high decibel of chatter dominated the dining area.

An orange tray with two double-double cheeseburgers, an order of home fries and a chocolate shake was being slowly savored by Gary Bub while Arney looked on. Bub was eating with his right arm. His left was in a sling and strapped to his body. This inconvenience didn't slow him down. The recovering police Sergeant was in ecstasy. After a week of hospital food this was heaven.

He spoke between bites. "So, what's the latest on the Fick case? Any further along?" He made a slight belch as he stuffed a few more fries into his mouth.

Arney grinned. "Two stalwart representatives from the FBI arrived a few days ago and they've made me a consultant. One of them is an old college buddy of mine. We played football at UCLA."

Bub stopped eating and looked up. "Shit, I never knew you went to college."

Arney grabbed a fry. "Hey bud, I wouldn't be where I am today without all that higher learning."

Bub went plowing through burger number two. "There's one hell of a recommendation for education." They laughed.

Arney's cell went off. It was too noisy in the dining area. He jumped up and went outside. Gary watched him through the window as he took the call. His friend's face turned grave.

Arney returned to the table. 'Well I've got some good news and some bad news. Which do you want first?"

Bub wiped his mouth. "Give me the bad news first then I can have dessert."

Arney grinned. "You're off this case, even in our agreed to unofficial capacity."

The donut loving lawman started to get pissed. 'What the hell do mean by that Blackburrn? Who in the hell just called? I'm not stopping until I find the SOB who shot me and that's final!"

"Well that's just it, dude. The person who shot you just committed suicide with her partner. You were right. It was a woman. I had a chat with her lesbian lover two days ago. The highway patrol just found them both up in the mountains with a bullet in each of their brains. Case closed on your side my man."

Gary Bub stared at Arney. After a few moments he began to nod his head very slowly. "Gee, and I was looking so forward to beating the shit out of whoever shot me before they went downtown." He focused on a car coming out of the drive through lane. "I'm really depressed."

Arney sat up straight. "What can I do to help you out?"

Bub looked down at his empty tray. "Another double-double and a homemade lemonade would probably do the trick."

Arney headed for the counter.

Thirty-three

Long Beach was deluged with a pounding rain. The barrage of water falling on the roof of the garage was louder than a rock drummer. Zoltin Slim was impatient and getting a headache. This project was entering the second week and everything seemed to come to a halt. He was tired of playing nursemaid.

Another thing that was preying on his mind was Dee Dee. Yesterday when the newspapers reported the death of Victor Gastaldi she disappeared. She should have been back by now. Just what the fuck is going on anyway?

When Zoltin set out to track down Dee the light rain he first encountered on the road turned into a torrent. He took his Harley back to the garage to wait it out.

He slept in the chair that his partner normally occupied and when he awoke, his back was killing him. It was eight in the morning: he had expected Dee by now. He was way pissed. Several calls to Dee's cell went straight to voicemail.

Every day he pilfered the morning paper from the neighbors who were out of town and sat in the patio with a cup of coffee and a cigarette;

his normal breakfast. Zoltin read the article slowly. He bit into his toothpick so hard he stabbed himself in the cheek. The slight pain woke him up.

Dee Dee had committed suicide with her lesbian girlfriend and as it turns out, Dee was the one who shot the cop at the Hilton a week and a half ago. His partner had become anxious around that time, and now he knew why she'd gone to L.A. With Dee out of the picture it was dropped in his lap to handle the so-called kidnap victim twenty four/seven.

No good. It was time to get nasty. This was looking like amateur night.

Zoltin whipped out his cell phone and speed dialed Ballantyne. He knew one thing for sure: he'd disappear before he'd go down.

He'd been uneasy about this job from the getty-up. He couldn't put it together in his head. So many things didn't make sense and without a ransom note or at least a demand, what in the hell was this whole thing about? Due to the demands on his time he was feeling more like the prisoner than the guard.

The rain stopped. He took out a fresh toothpick and headed for his Harley.

CHAPTER THIRTY-FOUR

Thirty-four

Half-way home from dropping off Gary Bub at his apartment Arney got a call from Chris asking him to meet him in the coffee shop of his hotel. When Arney arrived he found Chris munching slowly on a mid-afternoon breakfast. Chubbs wasn't there. "Where's your partner?"

"He's downtown checking over the evidence bags." Chris seemed distracted. "So, how's your buddy Gary Bub? Is he recovering?"

Arney glanced away from their booth. "Yeah, I picked him up and dropped him off at his apartment. I think he's got a good chance of a damn near full recovery."

"Listen Blackburn, you know we've been following you for a while."

Arney was all attention. "Have I been a good boy?

Chris laughed. "Don't take it that way. Because of your connection with Gastaldi and the Fick kidnapping the Bureau demanded to see who you're keeping company with."

Chris was dying for a cigarette. "How long have you known Abe Meyers?"

Arney laughed. "Your boys don't miss a thing, eh?" He signaled the waiter to bring him a coffee cup. "I've known Abe for about five years. I saved his kid from a deadly beating in a bar in Beverly Hills."

112

Chris rubbed his eyes. "We've been working with Abe for a long time. He's one of the private citizens on the board of our Art Crimes Division at the Bureau. So I imagine you asked him if he had any idea who in the private sector might be behind the kidnapping?"

Arney poured the last of the coffee. "Indeed I did. When I told him it was Fick's granddaughter, I also mentioned Fick's uncle the Nazi architect under Hitler's wing." Arney took the last piece of toast. "That's when he shut down."

Chris grabbed his notebook. "So, that was it? He wouldn't co-operate?"

Arney knew this was probably a trick question. The FBI agents were probably watching him when Abe's chauffeur handed him the envelope. "Not at first, but an hour or so later he had a list delivered to me at my house."

"You don't happen to have that list handy right now, do you?"

With a big smile the P.I. reached into his pocket and pulled out Abe's list. He handed it to Chris. "All household names; as famous as they get."

Chris studied the list slowly. When his eyes reached one name he smiled. "All, except one." His cell phone went off. It was Chubbs. Chris told him to get back here pronto. Chris gave Arney a wink. "...More coffee?"

Chubbs returned to his room.

The list that Abe Meyers had offered up was truly as Arney had described it. A "Who's, Who of Hollywood": some of the best known actors, writers and directors on the scene today. Chris got all excited when he read the name Madeline Steinman. He wouldn't say why but asked Chubbs to check the backgrounds of the others to find out how many had family in Europe during World War II. Chubbs logged on then decided to lie down and rest for a few minutes.

His life with the Bureau was non-stop.

Carlos Portman Gonzales was always aware of his physical condition. He had been a big man ever since high school. Working out every day was natural. Now that he was in his late thirties, he truly felt in his prime. He thought that there was something unique about a man approaching middle-age: there's still a good deal of muscle and drive left, yet you've also added a few decades of experience to your tool kit and you're not as likely to make any more dumb moves.

Chris was like an older brother. They spent more time together than most married couples. Maybe that's why Chubbs was feeling a little off the past few weeks.

Ariel George, a female FBI Agent Chris had gone through training with at Quantico two decades ago showed up unexpectedly at the American Embassy in Nice to join them on their last case. It was as if they had been waiting for each other, waking up from a long dream.

They became an item immediately but Chris, in his normal private way, never talked about their relationship. Chubbs often noticed when the two men were on the street that Chris would get a call and move away with a smile on his face: the timbre of his voice changing from the stiff Special Agent's monotone, to that of a man about to slobber all over himself.

Chubbs was happy for him, yet, in moments like these, alone in another non-descript hotel room, he began to wonder if there was someone waiting out there somewhere, about to surprise him, to put back what's missing—to offer food for his soul, a fresh reason to smile.

His momentary personal reflection was interrupted by a call from Chris to tell him they were going to see Abe Myers today. Chubbs put himself back in gear: just enough time for a quick morning workout.

His personal life would have to take a number and wait in line.

Thirty-five

Chris called Chubb's room. No answer. Tried his cell. Ditto.

A few minutes later Chubbs knocked on the door. He had just returned from jogging all over downtown L.A.. "Wow, this city must have been something else eighty years ago. Some of the pre-war buildings are wonderful examples of Art Nouveau architecture. They've really rebuilt the area since I was at UCLA: new restaurants, boutiques, living spaces. Man it's fantastic! "

Chris said nothing, just staring at his partner.

Chubbs smiled, understanding the unspoken. "...Got it right here, Chief." He took out an envelope and returned to his room to shower and shave.

In the silence of solitude, Chris concentrated on the research Chubbs did on Abe's list.

The one name that required no background research was Madeline Steinman. Chris was very familiar with her. He had sat enraptured at her lecture in the early eighties at the New York School of Fine Arts. Chris had experienced the high-priestess of art restoration up close and personal on that occasion. She held an open conference for all in attendance after

115

her talk: a chance to pick the brain of the leading authority in her field. He had a clear recollection of that event. She could not be involved in the Fick kidnapping. Besides, she must be nearly ninety years old!

But then why did Abraham Meyers include her? Several of the celebrities on Abe's list, including Ms. Steinman, had relatives who had been in one of the Nazi concentration camps. Abe must know or at least have suspected that one or more of their descendants may be behind the kidnapping. Tired of waiting around for International laws to kick in, it is probable that Industry vigilantes amongst the ARCA group lost sight of reality deciding to transform what they put on screen into real time.

The veteran FBI Special Agent was wondering if Stephanie Fick was still breathing, and if she was, how much longer she would be? Time was always the enemy in a kidnapping. Abductors were mentally unbalanced to begin with: as the pressure increased with the passage of time their actions could become violent toward their captive. Chris knew he needed to assemble the known facts and try to put together a picture that would lead them to the Stephanie Fick as soon as possible.

Then without warning that chill around his neck and shoulders crept in. He closed his eyes, and in a rush of images he began to put the pieces together. "That's it!" He exclaimed to an empty room.

A teenage Ezekiel Fick was guided to Madeline Steinman by his uncle who must at least have known her or more than likely, had been close to her shortly after the war ended. He told her about the slashed Monets and she couldn't resist repairing them. Since they were not really known to exist, there was no criminal act, just the pure joy of restoring the mutilated works of one the world's most prized Impressionist painters.

Ezekiel must have gone to Paris where she worked on the canvases. Ms. Steinman probably kept one for a fee. Afterwards, Ezekiel Fick found discreet buyers who knew what they were getting and were willing to pay. He took it from there and built his fortune: a pretty decent accomplishment.

Somehow those renegade Hollywood members of ARCA found out about Fick and discovered Roderick, one of Hitler's pets, was his uncle. They drew their own conclusions.

They assumed that the billionaire must have a stash of artwork gifted to him by his uncle after the war. Due to their faulty facts they abducted an innocent party.

Chris moved out onto the balcony puffing hard on a cigarette, staring down at the traffic in downtown L.A., wondering where everyone was going, and why?

Thirty-six

Danny Ballantyne sat across from Zoltin at the diner in Long Beach.

Mr. Slim had shot a maximum dose of morphine into Stephanie before he left her alone. Without Dee Dee around he couldn't take the chance of straying too far away from the stash-house without his captive doped up to the hilt.

The henchman slipped a quarter into the jukebox and Miles Davis oozed out of the speakers. The volume was adequate to muffle their conversation.

Zoltin Slim gave Danny one of his ice-cold stares. "So, tell me, what in the fuck do we do now?"

Danny stretched his hands out across the table. "I believe that the woman you hired to care for the girl has committed suicide, along with her girlfriend." Ballantyne looked around the room. "Law enforcement is convinced that this woman is also the person who shot the cop thinking he was me?"

Zoltin took out a fresh toothpick.

Danny continued. "And I just found out her brother was Victor Gastaldi and that he was murdered two days ago? Do I have my facts straight?"

Zoltin caught the waitress's eye. He ordered a chicken fried steak with mashed and a Schlitz. He then reloaded the juke box with several cuts from his hero, Miles.

When the music began again Zoltin took over. "I thought that it was your boys who took care of Gastaldi."

Danny folded his hands on the table. 'I would have been happy to have arranged that, but I didn't have anything to do with it."

Zoltin thought that last statement over for a moment. "You see my friend, I'm not a very patient man. The fucking wheels are coming off the cart. This job has got to be resolved within forty-eight hours—period!"

Danny stood up on his hind legs. 'You threatening me, Slim? That would not be a very wise move on your part." He heard the click from under the table. He knew what it was.

"It's pointed right into your crotch, Ballantyne." The smile on Zoltin's face would have cracked a mirror. "And oh yes....I would do it right here, right now and be gone in ten seconds, calling 911 and telling them all about you and the cute little girl you're hiding out a few blocks away."

Zoltin lowered the hammer. His meal had arrived. He took a swig of beer. "I know you're one of those tough guys from the windy city." He cut a bite of his steak and held it up in the air on his fork. He pointed it in Danny's direction. "We do this deal now motherfucker before I do something you'll be sorry for." He smiled that smile before he took his first bite.

Danny watched Zoltin in silence while he ate. He now understood that his employee was a real basket case and could go off-line at any moment.

It was time to get in touch with the old man and move this ship out of port.

The sixties glass paneled house Danny was renting above Sunset Boulevard in the Hollywood Hills had the perfect location. It offered a view or the entire L.A. basin as well as the Pacific Ocean on a clear day. Even when the smog was so thick you could cut it with a knife, the heavens could be seen at night.

Ballantyne reclined near the swimming pool with a drink in one hand and his cell in the other. He might buy the house when this was over.

He'd talked with Fick and the old man was ready to deal. Of course, Danny knew that he would more than likely call the Feds and whoever else is working this case to put them on the alert, but that didn't matter. The Chicago big shot had a fool-proof- plan. By the time the next day had seen the sun and moon he'd be set for life and no one would be the wiser. He knew how to deal with Zoltin; that was a piece of cake.

He would also need to deal with his old high school chum who helped set the ball in motion. That thought made him laugh. When law enforcement started to poke around to see who was behind the kidnapping the bread crumbs would lead to Mr. Academy Awards. Who in the hell did he think he was? He made movies. He dealt with fantasy twenty-four hours a day. Danny's world was the real one. In fact, if he wanted to go to the trouble he could blackmail his old buddy for years to come. But that wouldn't be necessary. No one in the world could possibly guess what the real deal was all about and who was behind it. The Chicago gangster couldn't stop smiling. Soon he would be far away, laying low for a year or so.

His secret partner in this escapade had it all figured out to the last detail. He knew he could rely totally on their expertise and insider information. Even a portion of Fick's fortune would be enough to support him lavishly until the day he dropped.

The gangster from the windy city went inside to change and get ready for a day trip to Long Beach. As soon as he finished this little piece of business he could focus totally on the final stage and the reward it would bring.

As he climbed into the van he dialed his partner to make sure they were on schedule. He could tell by the confidence in their voice that it would soon be over. At the bottom of the driveway he looked back at the house and smiled.

Thirty-seven

Chris had just received a text from the surveillance crew watching Blackburn. Conchita Morales was stashed at his home. Chris and Chubbs would have to pay Arney a visit.

Chris wasn't sure what he thought about the possible involvement of Hollywood personalities in the kidnapping. If he was in their place he might feel the frustration of knowing how much their families in Europe had suffered during the war: not only the lives taken but also the loss of treasured artifacts, some of which may have been handed down for generations.

The scary thing about it was the ego factor. Did they think their fame would provide a protective shield against the consequences of such an act? If one or two of Hollywood's blockbuster icons were in on the kidnapping at some level, believing that Ezekiel Fick possessed a collection of stolen art works from the Third Reich, then why would they delay notifying the old man of their demands and pushing for an exchange? It would certainly be to their advantage to get in and get out as quickly as possible to prevent discovery: why increase the chance of spending the rest of their lives locked away?

Fame, politics, power and money: the marriages that drives the world forward for better or for worse.

Chubbs adjusted his tie in the hotel room mirror. He stared at his image frozen by the reflection.

He was having another moment of dealing with his insides. It happened often lately even if he tried to sidestep the emotional trail he still found himself walking.

All these years his job with the Bureau had taken most of his time. Except for the occasional casual date for dinner, no time spent with the opposite sex had turned him around. He was a man of great sensitivity and feelings. His size and strength belied his emotional nature.

He shot one last glance at himself while putting on his holster and badge. He and Chris were headed out to bust his old friend for harboring a witness.

This was not promising to be a fun day.

Arney was mindlessly staring out the window at the lake sipping on a cup of French roast while Conchita was getting dressed. He wasn't sure how the day would unfold until he spied the unmarked county car pulling up to the curb. Chris and Chubbs were heading up the walk for the front door. Before they knocked, Arney slipped down the hallway and told Conchita to stay put and not to make a noise.

He greeted them with a smile. "…Yo Feds, whatcha doin' in this neck of the woods?" Chubbs smiled. Chris answered.

"Well we just stopped by to see if you might offer us a cup of your legendary French roast and that you might also cough up an extremely important witness to the Gastaldi murder which may have a bearing on the Fick kidnapping." Chris smiled. Chubbs frowned.

"Come on in gentlemen, coffee's on the stove and I'll gather up that package for you while you're pouring." Arney went to the bedroom and quickly told Conchita the situation. The smile left her face. "Do I have to go with these guys?"

Arney stroked her hair. "Believe me it's the best thing to do right now.

I don't know how they found out that you're here, but that's what they get paid for. As far as I know you're not a suspect. They just want to talk to you. Go downtown for an interview and call me when you're done. I'll come and pick you up." Arney smiled. "I'll take you out for Mexican in Echo Park."

Conchita stuck her tongue out and gathered up her things.

Who can truly predict the reaction of one person meeting another, no matter what the circumstances?

Chubbs Gonzales was standing in the kitchen when Conchita glided out of the hallway. Chubbs turned to greet her and he felt like a thousand volts of electricity had shot through his body. Arney introduced Chris first and he immediately informed her that she was being taken into custody as a witness in regards to the murder of Victor Gastaldi.

Chris then introduced her to Chubbs. She smiled at him as if they knew each other but hadn't seen each other in a long time. "Olá, Señor."

Chubbs tried to control himself but his smile burst out and filled the room. "Olá, to you Senorita." Arney and Chris looked at each other then everyone headed toward the open door.

Arney toasted the three with his coffee cup. "You folks have a nice day and keep me posted."

Chris asked Chubbs to take Conchita to the car. He turned to Arney. "I'm not done with you yet Blackburn. You mind telling me why you had a witness stashed at your home?"

Arney took the coffee cup from Chris's hand. "I think the little lady is in serious danger Clarke. Whoever took out Gastaldi just might be trying to make a clean sweep of all of his associates. She's a hooker, but she was also Gastaldi's steady." Arney posted a slight smile.

"Take care of her bud, she's one in a million."

Thirty-eight

The normal routine of a witness interview includes the stock forwarding remarks which concern the importance of telling the truth and the slating of recording devices. Chris and Chubbs sat across from Conchita in one of the interview rooms in the downtown precinct. Chubbs was having a difficult time focusing. Chris noticed but didn't comment. The interview took up most of an hour and aside from some details regarding Victor Gastaldi's personal life, there was not much to be gained from the hooker's testimony.

She hadn't been with Victor since the night before his murder. Yes, she worked for the notorious Bigelow brothers but had no intention of going back to that life or the brothers for that matter now that Victor was dead.

Arney had offered her protection when she showed up on his doorstep after finding out about the murder. She had been to Arney's house once before under orders from Victor to return his gun after a failed attempt to shake Victor down.

Chubbs had remained silent throughout the event, taking some notes but not contributing one question. When their time was concluded, Chris went down the hall to Chief McCreary's office to see if the LAPD had any questions for the ex-lover of Victor Gastaldi.

124

Chubbs spoke now that the two were alone. "I'm sure that this has not been easy for you Ms. Morales. You've obviously lead a tough life. I hope things get better for you when all of this is over."

Chubbs was surprised by her response. "And you, mister FBI, have you had it that easy?"

Just then Chris came through the door. "Stay put, Ms. Morales, the locals want to have a few words with you then after that you'll be free to go." Chris looked at Chubbs. "Give the young lady your card, partner, in case she has anything more to offer or needs our help in some way."

Chubbs handed her his card pointing out the cell-phone number. They said their goodbyes and Chris and Chubbs headed out for lunch.

Chubbs seemed to be lacking his normal voracious appetite. He sat opposite Chris shuffling his food around the plate in silence. Chris set down his knife and fork.

"Okay partner, give. What's up? I know she's too young to have also been a friend of yours at UCLA."

Chubbs appeared to have not heard Chris. "I just don't get it, boss. How does someone like that end up the way she is? I can feel that she's not an idiot. I mean, she would be perfect if only she wasn't…"

Chris jumped in. 'If only she wasn't a whore? Jesus Christ Chubbs, come back. A hooker is a hooker because that's the way she goes. She didn't arrive at a crossroads and say to herself, gee, let's see, shall I be a rocket scientist or a prostitute?"

Chubbs became defensive. "Yeah, but how in the fuck do we know what drove her to that place? I could have been a gang leader in the hood but I ended up as an FBI agent. I had a supportive family with good moral values. What if she was more or less forced into it?" Chubbs shoved his plate away from him. "I know, I know, I'm a big boy and the experience of my job should not let things like this affect me." He downed the rest of his coke. "I can't explain it."

Chris gave his partner a long look and a warm smile. "Maybe it doesn't have anything to do with what she is or who you are. For whatever reason, something clicked when you met her and for that my friend, there's no explanation that I can come up with that would be worth listening to."

Chris signaled the waitress for the bill. "In the meantime, we've got a date to talk with Abe Meyers to see if he can shed any light in our direction. Copy?"

Chubbs left the tip.

Thirty-nine

A two century old folio edition of the History of the Crusades was spread out on Abe Meyer's desk when Chris and Chubbs entered the room. The old man was totally absorbed. His butler made a slight cough to let Abe know he had company. He turned around with a glazed look in his eyes and welcomed the two Agents. Pointing to the book he said, "The history of my people is intertwined with medieval Catholic Crusaders who protected them after Saladin conquered Jerusalem. It's a fascinating view of the ancient world." He closed the cover gently and offered each a chair. "It's amazing. The same religious and social issues that were prevalent in that region centuries ago are still with us." Abe looked at Chris. "I don't suppose that would be of much interest to you two at the moment?" He lit his pipe.

Chris spoke. "We appreciate your taking the time to see us. Actually, we just have one question."

Abe smiled at Chubbs. "I would imagine that it has to do with the list I sent to Arney. Perhaps a name or two was of interest to you people?"

Chubbs smiled back. "Every name on the list was interesting."

Abe fumbled with his lighter. "Yes. I thought that they might be."

Chris focused. "What's your relationship with Madeline Steinman? She certainly is no part of the Hollywood set."

A twinkle crossed Abe's eyes as he set his pipe down in the ashtray and put his hands behind his head. "You know of her, Agent Clarke?"

Chris locked onto Abe's eyes. "Yes, and you know that I do because you're aware of my background in art restoration and evaluation of antiquities because you are a member of the FBI's Art Theft association. My question is why was she included on your list? Does it have to do with the missing Monets that Fick's uncle left him when his father died? Do you know for a fact that Roderich sent Ezekiel to her to have them restored?" Chris watched the old man fidget.

Chris continued. "Because if you do, then all of these well-intentioned Hollywood-ites are in for a big surprise when they find out that there is nothing left of Fick's treasure, and in fact it was never part of a Nazi confiscated collection. Those Monet canvases were thought to be destroyed by the artist himself in 1926. Fick isn't liable for anything in regards to looted art works during the war. However, the renegade members of ARCA will be guilty of kidnapping an innocent human being and they will not be thinking about their next movie but their next move, more than likely to a Federal lockup."

Abe's shoulders slumped as his wing-backed chair seemed to be swallowing him. "My good fellows, it is possible that a few of the actors, directors, writers, producers and composers that make up the bulk of why Hollywood is Hollywood might be tempted to kidnap a relative of someone who profited from the suffering of their families during the war." Abe began to shuffle papers on his desk concentrating on the desk top.

"Occasionally an actor I represented over the years thought themselves to be above the law because of their fame. One seemingly brave and impetuous moment could bring the world crashing down on them." Abe folded his arms across his chest. "It saddens me to think that anyone in our group would go to such lengths to revenge the past."

The old man stood, clearly indicating that their time together was over. He smiled his practiced show-business grin. "I'm very tired… if you gentlemen will excuse me."

The butler returned as if on cue. Abe offered a slight wave.

Chris and Chubbs stood. Chris went over to shake Abe Meyer's hand. "I certainly hope that if you think of anything else that may aid us in this investigation that you will not hesitate to get in touch with us." Chris offered the aging ex-Hollywood agent a warm smile. "Your list was a very welcome gesture and we thank you for it."

Abe Meyers offered the two Agents his authentic smile. 'I sincerely hope that this situation is resolved quickly for the sake of Stephanie Fick. If I have made a minor contribution, it is all the thanks I need."

Chubbs broke in with a question out of left field. "Is it true that you were Dustin Hoffman's agent when he was offered the role in *Tootsie* and that you advised him to turn it down?"

Chris gave Chubbs a sideways glance. Abe laughed.

"Stop by some time Agent Gonzales and I'll tell you the whole story."

CHAPTER FORTY

Arney went downtown to pick up Conchita. She seemed changed after her interview with Chris and Chubbs. She stared out the passenger side window without a word as they crawled along Second Avenue in commuter traffic.

Arney checked his rear view mirror. "How'd it go?"

Conchita paused before answering. "Okay."

He laughed. "I'm not sure I can handle all those details."

A sixteen wheeler let off its air-horn right behind them and it startled the pair. Conchita was shocked back into reality.

"Can you drop me off at my mom's house in Echo Park?"

This request threw Arney for a moment but he recovered quickly. "Sure...no prob."

The young hooker gave him directions saying little else on the way. "I just need to be by myself for a while and put things together. I'll be safe with ma Madre. No one even knows I have a mother in L.A."

Arney pulled up to a property off of Echo Park Boulevard on Avalon Street. Conchita reached over and gave him a peck on the cheek and hurriedly exited. He watched her go down the driveway and disappear toward a house on the back of the lot.

———•◆———

Chubbs was relaxing in his hotel room watching cable when his cell went off. He answered it without checking caller ID. "…Gonzales here." There was a brief silence that got his attention, then a female voice.

"This is Conchita Morales, is it a good time to talk?"

Chubbs shut off the television and sat up in bed. "Yeah, you okay? Something wrong?"

She giggled. "No, I was just wondering what you were doing for dinner tonight? There's something I didn't tell you today."

Chubbs smiled. "Can't you tell me over the phone?"

Conchita sighed. "I understand. Sorry to bother you…"

Chubbs broke in. "Not a problem. Listen, this sounds important. I'll call you back in five minutes, alright?"

An hour later Chubbs and Conchita were seated at Barrigan's Mexican restaurant on Sunset in Echo Park. They ordered. Chubbs found the petite Latina to be as bright as a laser during their conversation.

As they chatted Conchita gave no clue about what she had to say that was relevant to the case. Coffee arrived. After the first sip Chubbs spoke. "Okay, what gives? Do you have more info concerning Victor's death?"

Conchita stirred her coffee while staring down at the table. "I'm afraid that I haven't been completely honest with you."

Chubbs took an official posture, sitting up straight and folding his hands in front of him on the table. "Well that's understandable under the circumstances. There is a lot of stress and pressure when being interviewed by law enforcement personnel. The important thing is that you've contacted us again and I'm sure that whatever you have remembered concerning the case will be most useful."

Conchita squirmed in her chair while glancing around the room. "It's not like that. It doesn't have anything to do with Victor's death." She started to laugh while shaking her head in disbelief. "I can't believe I'm about to say what I'm going to say."

Chubbs tried to calm her down. 'It's alright, Ms. Morales, just let it out and we'll deal with it."

Conchita burst out laughing which caught the attention of the other diners. She retrieved her composure. "No, I'm afraid that you won't believe me. This has all been a big mistake. I'd like to go now if it's okay with you." She began to gather up her things.

"Excuse me, but I don't understand what's going on here. You called me under the pretext that you had additional information pertinent to the investigation and now you have nothing to say?" Chubbs continued with some heat. "Listen, this job is tough enough and I really don't have time to waste." He motioned for the waiter to bring the check.

Unexpectedly Conchita reached over and grabbed his hand while he was distracted. Chubbs snapped his head back to face her smile. "It's you. Something happened to me when we met this morning. I know it's completely insane but I feel like I've known you for a long time and I don't get it."

Chubbs melted. His Cheshire-cat grin exploded and he squeezed her hand gently.

The big fellow's mind was racing at a million miles per hour. He could feel the blood coursing through his veins as if it were being pumped mechanically. His chest expanded and for the first time in his career with the Bureau he wished that he were anything but an FBI agent. Right now he wanted to be a simple man who could just run full tilt with his feelings without thinking about the consequences.

But a few moments later his years of experience kicked in. He retrieved his official demeanor. "Look, you're still a key witness and that's how things are at the moment. Let's get you back home." He winked. "Even an FBI Agent gets to have a date once in a while. Let's just take it a day at a time and see where it goes…Okay?"

Conchita gave Chubbs a look that he would carry in his memory bank forever no matter what the future held.

Within minutes they pulled up to the curb on Avalon Street. The front house was dark. Chubbs offered to walk her to the back but she declined, reaching over to give him a moist kiss on the cheek and then ran down the driveway.

FBI special Agent Carlos Portman Gonzales pulled away from the curb in a daze and drove back to the hotel averaging around fifteen miles an hour. Impatient drivers were honking at him all the way back. He didn't notice.

Forty-one

The TV was blaring. Chubbs knocked on Chris's door. Chris gave that *gotcha* smile to his partner. "Well, well, well, if it isn't my swinging bachelor buddy all aglow from his evening out."

"Fuck you." Chubbs burst into the room and stood by the windows staring at the L.A. skyline. It shocked Chris.

Chris shut off the television. "Alright, I'm sorry partner, you didn't deserve that. I know it's been a dry patch for a long time and…"

Chubbs turned to face Chris. "And what…? I finally meet someone for the first time in years that knocks me out and who is she? A dime hooker at least fifteen years younger than me and to top things off, she's tied up with our current case and has probably been ballin' Arney and I have to stand here and listen to your smart-ass remarks on top of it?"

Chris moved past the moment. "I just had some fresh coffee sent up. Let's have a cup. There's been some interesting developments since you headed out tonight."

Chubbs sat down. "Sorry, chief, I just had a low moment.

Chris pulled out a folder. "You have nothing to apologize for amigo. Here's where we stand."

—————•◆•—————

"After our talk with Abe Meyers I think you and I agree that Ballantyne was engaged by someone or some group connected to ARCA in the film industry to kidnap Stephanie Fick."

Chubbs quipped back. "I agree, but there is always the possibility that private parties, not affiliated with the industry, could have done the deed. If it is film industry persons, they would be risking everything. Do we have any idea who?"

Chris poured the coffee. "No, but unless they come forward we never will. I think that was what Abe was trying to tell us. His list could be twelve names or two hundred, it wouldn't matter. Only an attack of guilt might expose our conspirators. To some, the act itself might be their reward; goal accomplished. It only shows that certain members of ARCA, particularly those who have a Hollywood career, may be tempted to take the law into their own hands to get back their families' stolen property."

Chubbs thought. "So then, after Ballantyne arrived in L.A. he decided to go for more than the kidnapping. He wanted to take over Gastaldi's drug operation in his spare time which led to Sgt. Bub getting shot at the Hilton last week. Right? And that's where Arney fits in. Gastaldi twisted Arney's arm to track Ballantyne holding out the carrot that the Chicago mobster was connected to the kidnapping. But Arney was asked by Chief McCreary to tail Fick so he asked his police buddy Bub to keep an eye on Ballantyne."

Chris downed a coffee. "Check hike amigo. The two men looked enough alike that Gastaldi's sister who was trying to get back into her brother's good graces after he found out that she was a lesbian, decided to take Ballantyne out. She had a description of the gangster and where he was staying from her brother."

Chubbs looked up. "So how many other players do we have in this case? Gastaldi's dead. Dee Dee, who figures as one of the kidnappers or at least one of the captors holding the girl, committed suicide two days ago." Chubbs paused over his notes. " If Ballantyne was hired by parties responsible for the kidnapping, why hire a Chicago hood when there are plenty of bad guys in the L.A.? What the hell goes on here?"

Chris was staring into his coffee cup as if he were reading tea leaves. "What if Ballantyne was an old acquaintance of one of the Hollywood set. Maybe a high school chum that they ran into recently? We should look at a list of SAG members to see who was raised in Chicago!"

Chubbs broke in. "Wait a minute, chief." He scrolled through his BlackBerry. "I made a note as we were having our first talk with Arney. When he told us about those keys that Gastaldi gave him to research, didn't he say that a blind locksmith in Long Beach was the source?"

Chris poured the last dregs of coffee into his cup. "Yeah, I remember something like that: strange occupation for a blind man. What's the point?"

Chubbs beamed. "Well, the person who had those keys made might be the one we're looking for: keys to the deadbolts of a safe house in the area where they have the girl. That information may lead us to the Hollywood/Chicago connection."

Chris gulped the coffee. "Well how in the hell is a blind man going to help us identify our suspect? If he couldn't see…"

Chubbs cut in. "…He could hear! Maybe he heard the sound of a vehicle or some other audio clue about the customer to help us identify him. It's worth a try anyway."

Chris saluted Chubbs with his coffee cup. "Right on, my man. Let's rouse Arney and get the name and number."

Chubbs continued to beam. "…way ahead of you—oh mighty-one. When Arney gave us his name, I found his info on the net. We can call Joseph Lobo first thing in the morning."

Forty-two

The blind locksmith had good ears. When Chubbs finished the call he went on the Net.

Chris waited. "Got anything?"

Chubbs was finishing his search. "Sure do. Mr. Lobo heard the sound of a Harley Davidson before the guy walked in and right after he left."

Chris yawned and stretched. "Well that should narrow it down to a few thousand suspects."

Chubbs laughed. "I think we did better than that with this witness. His hearing is so sensitive that he can tell the difference in Harleys as to the model and year the engine belongs to." Chubbs laughed. 'Lobo told me that he could hear a duck fart from a hundred yards on a foggy day.'

Chris chuckled. "So what's the skinny?"

Chubbs checked his notes. "Well Lobo believes that the motor was from a KH model, sounding like one from the fifties or sixties. I'm running a tag right now to see how many of these models are registered with the DMV in Long Beach."

A knock on the door announced breakfast. Chubb's face was concentrated. "It looks like there are only about a half-dozen KH models from those two decades in Long Beach." Chubbs switched to the Bureau laptop and fed in the names of the owners. "Got him!" Chris moved over to the screen. Chubbs glowed. "There's a dude named Zoltin Slim who's seen some jail time. Partner, I'm putting my money on this perp as our man with the hideout and the girl."

Chris slapped Chubbs on the back. When the scene in the video they viewed at Ezekiel Fick's home, showed Stephanie Fick bound to a bed, Chris noticed that the interior of the room seemed more like a garage than a room in a house. The only windows were centered on the far wall and there was acoustic pink fiberglass insulation protruding along the edge of the shot.

Might be a garage door.

Long Beach wasn't that huge. Chris would get Mac's people to check with the Long Beach Police department to request them to search the area for vacant craft-style houses with un-attached garages at the back of the property.

It wouldn't take that much time. That wood-plank style of architecture was popular in the region during the twenties through the Second World War. Many of these structures had been torn down over the years to be replaced with modern multi-dwelling apartment units. Today, there would be select neighborhoods in the area that would still boast the refurbished homes. One of these properties could be hiding the victim.

Forty-three

The back house down the driveway on Avalon Street in Echo Park was dark. Due to its location, none of the neighbors had a view of the occupants. The man seated on the enclosed veranda was smoking a Cuban cigar. He gently blew perfect smoke rings and watched them drift off. The screen door creaked open and a woman stepped out with a tray sporting a bottle of Jose Cuervo Gold, and two shot glasses with lime and salt. The man smiled. "Now there's a great idea. …Time for a little celebration Senorita?"

She set the tray down and bent over to give the man a kiss. He spied her breast and pinched her nipple. She laughed and sat down next to him. He put his arm around her.

"Everything go okay tonight?"

Conchita laughed. "You bet. The entire police force thinks I'm in love with them."

"That's my girl." Bernie Needlbaum poured two shots of tequila. They toasted each other with interlocked arms and gulped it down. He took a long drag off his cigar. He stroked her hair. "Pretty soon we'll be in your native country on a permanent vacation. These clowns have no idea who they're fucking with."

Conchita poured herself another shot then slithered down from the couch to her knees and unzipped his pants.

Forty-four

All was still inside the library of Ezekiel Fick's mansion except for the noise of a crackling fire. The billionaire hung up the phone slowly. His eyes were caught in a trance by the flames' flicker.

Stephanie would be returned. That was all he cared about. The plan was a basic one as it had been explained to him by the stranger just now. The kidnapper would bring Stephanie to a specified location and they would make an exchange: simple as that.

Now the elderly billionaire needed to think about what to do.

The kidnappers had abducted Stephanie on the premise that he had a collection of priceless works of art confiscated by the Nazis.

In truth, the thirteen Monet canvasses which his uncle had let him had all been sold before 1970. The money had been invested wisely in industrials and commodities. Hanging wasn't good enough for these people: to have assumed that he was an ex-Nazi or for what he could only imagine that his innocent granddaughter had been through in the past weeks.

He knew what he would do for the exchange. He had removed seven paintings from his personal collection of nineteenth and twentieth century art, worth millions, and would offer them as if it were from what Roderich had left him. How would they know?

Now he had only one problem. Should he inform the FBI and the mayor, or just go it alone and tell them that Stephanie had been mysteriously returned to his home in the middle of the night? What about those individuals who made the video; those that know so much about his past? Will they leave him alone now? Is he safe to live out the rest of his days in peace?

He searched around in his desk for the card of the FBI agent and also the phone number of Arnold Blackburn. He held each in one of his hands. Who should he call? Who would understand and help without any judgment?

The old man dialed Arney and waited.

The private detective was deep in thought when his cell went off. He almost didn't answer it. At the last moment he flipped it open. "…Yeah, what?"

The voice on the other end of the line was old and weak. "Mr. Blackburn?"

Arney barely recognized Fick. "You don't sound very well. Are you okay?"

The old man took a breath. "I just got a call…"

Arney interrupted. "They're ready to deal?"

Fick answered cautiously. "I think so. At least they've made a proposition to meet and exchange."

"Did you call the Feds? They'll want to know ASAP."

The old man seemed unsure. 'I didn't know what to do. I called you. I don't really know why." He coughed. "Maybe it's because we are slightly alike—two independent bastards."

Arney smiled.

Fick jumped in with his former energy. "I can feel you thinking. The contact said no cops or I'd be picking her up in a bag!"

Arney attempted to reassure the old man. "It's a must-do but the two Feds you met are pros; they know what to do." Arney changed directions. "Tell me Zeke, how old do you think the voice was? Thirties, forties, fifties or beyond?

The billionaire thought about it. "I don't really know if I had to take a guess I'd say mid-forties."

Arney grabbed a cookie. "Okay, listen to me. When and where do they want to make the switch?"

Fick was all business now. "They said they would contact me within the next twenty four hours and give me the details."

Arney chanced it. "I assume they're not looking for cash. They want the remainder of the art collection your uncle left you decades ago, am I right?"

No response.

"Stay at home. Don't worry, the only one following you to the exchange will be me and don't forget I'm not a cop anymore so it doesn't break any of their rules."

Ezekiel Fick said he'd be waiting.

Arney hung up wondering if that would turn out to be true.

Forty-five

Seated in Arney's living room, Chris and Chubbs listened intently as he related his conversation with the Pasadena billionaire while the three of them stared out across the lake.

"So that's the way it is. We don't know who the hell called but it was probably this guy Zoltin you've fished up or Danny Ballantyne."

Chris snuffed out a smoke. "More than likely Ballantyne. He must be the one in charge. Zoltin is his hired hand. It's not helping that we don't know who instigated this plan." Chris stretched. "The main goal is, and always has been, to rescue the girl."

Chubbs was watching joggers grouped together circling the lake. "I still don't think we've got the full picture."

Arney poured some more French roast. "How's that, bud?"

Chubbs stood up and paced. "Well as I see it, there are still two more suspects that we haven't nailed. One would be that right-hand man of Gastaldi's, Bernie Needlebaum. After his high-powered lawyer posted bail Chief McCreary thinks that he's hiding out somewhere in L.A. I'm sure he knows as much about the kidnapping as Victor did. He probably has a plan of his own to get grandpa's stash. Even one Monet would set anyone up for life."

Chris jumped in. "Okay, so who's the other party?"

Chubbs smiled his Cheshire-cat smile. "I'm putting my money on Conchita."

Arney laughed. "You can't be serious? You're just pissed that I was there first."

Chubbs stood up. "That's a hell of a statement regarding a hooker." Chubbs became serious. "No, I'm not pissed, I'm focused." He sat back down facing his partners. "Look, when you took her to that house in Echo Park did she let you walk her to the back unit?"

Arney cleared his throat. "No, she said I didn't need to bother. Her mother was home."

Chubbs smiled again. "Well partner, when I took her there after dinner she didn't ask me to escort her either so I did a little background check." He pulled out his BlackBerry. "Conchita's mother passed away in two thousand and two. That would make it pretty hard for her to come home and give mommy a good night kiss."

Chris stood up and nodded to Chubbs. "How far are we from the house on Avalon Street?"

Chubbs prepared to leave. "Not more than ten minutes."

Chris called Chief Mac and asked to send back up to the Echo Park address. Arney felt like he was not in the loop. "So, should I just hang here and put another batch of cookies in the oven?"

Chris checked his service weapon. "I think it would be a good idea for you to go to Fick's address and make sure the old man isn't thinking about doing something stupid. We'll touch base with you as soon as we've cleared the house. If we find Needlebaum and Conchita together, we'll take them downtown and put them through the ringer."

No goodbyes were exchanged. The front door clicked shut and Arney felt an eerie calm.

He'd only spent two nights with the suspect but she knew him inside out. What a bitch life is.

Some people have what it takes and yet they're held back by their own fate, destiny or just plain stupidity.

Chubbs also recognized her qualities. Wow, is she ever slick. She made fools out of both of them.

---◆---

By the time Chris and Chubbs arrived at the scene, L.A. SWAT teams were in place. Everything was quiet. In the late afternoon the property was draped in shadows making it unclear as to if there was any activity in the house. All seemed quiet. The drapes on the windows that could be seen were drawn. All members of the force were in place. Chief McCreary stood nearby. "It's your call boys. They're your suspects. What do you want to do?"

They looked at each other and without speaking started to sneak down the driveway with their weapons drawn. Mac got on his walkie-talkie and let the SWAT Commander know what was going on. The team was on the ready.

The back house was cut off from the neighbors by a high fence and lots of trees. A gentle breeze was rustling the leaves. The gate stood slightly ajar. It was metal with criss-cross webbing. Chris motioned to Chubbs. The two agents approached cautiously. Chubbs was praying that the gate wouldn't squeak, giving them away. Chris pushed it open a few inches. It was silent. Neither had any idea how the property was set up. They crouched down and went through.

A cat meowed.

They froze for two seconds then staying low they approached the front of the structure. The house was of wood plank construction and had probably been built in the twenties. The porch was enclosed and faced Echo Park Boulevard. There was no view, just the constant rumble of passing traffic. Four steps led up to the screen door. Pointing at the wooden stairs Chubbs made a sign shaking his head. They were old and rotted. There would be no way to climb them without tipping off the occupants. Chris knew that there was a SWAT team member on all sides of the house. The two Agents winked at each other and silently mouthed the words— "Let's do it!"

Chris and Chubbs charged up the stairs smashed the screen door. Chubbs shouldered his way through the front door with Chris in tow. "FBI...put your hands on your head." There was no one in the front room. The duo motioned to each other and they started to clear the house. SWAT team members took out the back door charging through the kitchen. Within a few seconds the house was clear.

No one home.

They holstered their weapons. "What'da think, chief?" Chris heard Chubbs but wasn't ready with an answer. "I think our couple got word we were on the way or they're out having a romantic picnic in Echo Park."

Chubbs began poking around. "I'll be willing to bet that whoever was on the payroll from downtown to keep Gastaldi informed still has a job."

"Roger that, partner." Chris strolled through the house and returned to the front room. "Bed sheets are warm and there are clothes for both sexes. They ran out fast." Chris called Arney.

He picked up on the first ring. Arney shouted at Chris. "It looks like Fick is preparing for the worst. Jesus, he's got a set of short-barrel shotguns stashed in the trunk."

Chris got to the point. "I need you to remember if you can, what brand of cigarettes Bernie Needlebaum smoked?"

Arney jumped in. "…He didn't. He was a cigar smoker."

Chris stared at the ash tray full of cigar butts and told Arney to follow Fick and stay in touch all the way. Arney broke in. "Hold on, Fick just got another call and he's going back inside. Must be a change of plan."

Chris turned to Chubbs. "Great, now they've postponed the exchange. Fick was all packed up to go and now he's back in his house."

"Holed up in his castle, you mean." Chubbs grinned.

Bernie and Conchita were huddled together inside the boarded-up garage next to the back house. He couldn't believe that the Feds or the SWAT team hadn't checked it. Conchita's breathing was rapid below nervous eyes. Bernie had a spread of automatic weapons in front of him as if they were set up at a gun show. The front of the garage was nailed shut and the windows had been replaced with sheets of plywood. It looked un-accessible. Bernie had built a secret entrance for emergencies. Now it was being tested.

His informant downtown called just in time for the couple to hide.

Bernie was sweating. It was too quiet outside. He hadn't heard anyone give a command to disperse. His head froze in one position and his eyes darted around the room listening with all of the strength he had.

Nothing.

The cat meowed. Then it happened. All of the boarded up windows caved in at once as a half-dozen tear gas canisters crashed through, filling the room with a smoky haze.

Bernie didn't hesitate. He came out swinging, firing blindly with an automatic in each hand. Within seconds rounds of ammo came bursting back in his direction ten-fold to his barrage. He screamed in agony as Conchita watched his riddled body bounce up and down as if he were hip-hop dancing. She had crawled behind some metal barrels when the first sounds of invasion occurred. The walls of the garage were Swiss-cheesed in seconds. Conchita bit her tongue to stay quiet and calm. SWAT team officers stormed the structure and cuffed Needlebaum even though it was probable that his heart had stopped as he lay in a bloody pool.

Chubbs knew that Conchita couldn't have escaped. He marched to the back of the garage tossing away fifty gallon metal industrial barrels like they were Legos. She screamed and tried to escape but a bullet had found her and she could barely move. Chubbs grabbed her. She looked at him with a pleading expression but he paid no attention. He handed her to one of the female swat team members, not looking back.

Bernie was a goner. They're only hope for more info on the kidnapping was Conchita. Chris thought he now knew who had killed Victor. He just wasn't sure how she did it.

Forty-six

The black Mercedes SUV was packed and ready to go. Ezekiel Fick had the tools necessary to accomplish the job. No one was going to do this to him no matter what. He would be sure that Stephanie was safe and on her way with the police and then he would go into action. He checked his bullet-proof vest for comfort. His shoulder holster was guarding a Colt .380 Mustang— ideal for personal protection. He had bottled water, blankets, a first-aid-kit and food in the trunk alongside a pair of Remington over-under sawed off shotguns loaded to take down Kodiak Grizzlies.

He squeezed his cell phone so tightly he almost broke it. He put on his Blue Tooth ear piece and tossed the phone into the passenger seat. He could now handle all calls hands free. Any minute now his final instructions would arrive. He waited. His breathing had been heavy and hard. His pulse slowed down now that he knew he was prepared.

His Bluetooth activated. "Yes?"

The voice on the other end was not the same one from yesterday. "A dark blue Dodge van will meet you tomorrow at the entrance to Griffith Park off Vermont at exactly two o'clock." The caller waited for a response. "Do you understand?"

The old man was furious. "Just wait a god damn minute. You said the exchange was to take place today…why the delay?

In a calm tone the voice said, "Change of plans. Tomorrow at two and no law enforcement or the girl is toast." The line went dead.

Danny Ballantyne tossed his cell phone onto the passenger seat of the van. He was cruising the Harbor freeway south near the San Pedro exit heading for Long Beach. He stared out of the window at the clouds coming in off the ocean. They were brown with smog.

That afternoon, for the first time in his life Zoltin Slim was out of toothpicks. There wouldn't be any time to stop and buy some. He had just forty minutes to meet Danny, get the van, pick up Stephanie, and be off to Glendale. Danny said that he would be waiting at the safe-house with the girl packed up and ready to go when Mr. Slim arrived.

Zoltin, sans toothpick, fired up his Harley and headed down the alley in long Beach. The van was only a few blocks away and the key was sitting on top of the left front tire. Zoltin cruised by the Cherry Street diner and gave it a nod. Three minutes later he made a left hand turn on Parakeet Lane. Then it happened.

From out of nowhere a speeding van came up from behind the cyclist and rammed him, causing the massive two-wheeler to roll and flip with its rider. The bike came to a stop and people gathered. The rider didn't move. The van sped away before anyone thought to get a license number. An onlooker dialed 911 and soon a siren was heard in the near distance. Zoltin's skull was crushed.

A bystander commented. "Stupid fuck, he only had one of those fake helmets, barely legal."

True to form, Zoltin hated anything made past nineteen sixty-three. And died for it.

Forty-seven

The twenty-six year old prostitute woke up in a fog with her forehead feeling as if it were being crushed between two boulders. For a few seconds she didn't know where she was or what had happened. Her right arm was killing her. She tried to move her other arm but it was handcuffed to the bed. She had been here before. L.A. County general. A nurse was next to her and a uniformed officer was just outside the door.

She wasn't feeling her usual adrenaline of confidence. The image of Bernie's bullet-punctured body bordered by rivulets of blood made her sick. The room seemed to be turning like the Ferris wheel at Griffith Park. She knew that things couldn't be worse, but Conchita Morales was beyond her years in experience and cunning.

Her education had taken place on the streets of Los Angeles where she had graduated with honors. She started as a hooker at the age of twenty. In a short span of time she had seen it all. As both Arney and Chubbs had discovered, the woman, despite her serious faults, had depth of character and a shrewd, perceptive mind. Even now as she lay wounded in police custody, she was hatching a plan that might get her through all of this misery.

What the authorities didn't know was her secret ace-in-the-hole. Both Bernie and Victor had confided in her about the political payoffs that Victor kept up to date each month to keep the law at a distance. Victor was not only paying off the police department but he had a few of the local politicians in his pocket as well. They too enjoyed exotic substances, endless girls, and a convenient avenue to borrow large sums of cash which had no paper trail. Victor was always very accommodating to their needs.

Arney told her that the experts from LAPD crime scene investigation had gone through Victor's house several times but had only found drugs, cash and some weapons. Although it hurt, Conchita laughed when she thought of Victor's genius. All his files and records were on hard-drive CD discs in his collection of vintage cars. Four discs inserted in the CD players of four cars. The night she whacked him, she collected the discs and stored them in a safe place outside the house in Echo Park.

The image of killing Victor flooded her mind. When he found her having sex with his sister, he wigged out. Conchita knew the romance was over. She was a whore. She had sex with either gender for money. That was her life: man or woman, it was the cash that counted. When Dee Dee came to see Victor to try and make amends, Conchita was taking a shower and Dee Dee accidently walked into the bathroom. It was all over in ten minutes. Conchita left the woman breathing hard and took two fifties for her efforts. Just another day in the life, but Victor came through the bathroom door in full fury. Conchita ran out, half dressed, and returned two nights later to take care of Victor by the swimming pool. There were no witnesses, and she was free of his abuse. Where's the problem?

What would the next few days bring?

When she was close to recovery she knew they would attempt to prosecute her for…for what? What had she done? She was the girlfriend of two known felons and the lover of a private detective. She was a known hooker and had been up on those charges before but cleared by the Bigelow brothers' attorneys.

After her release she would pick up the files. A little blackmail for seven figures would set her up for life.

The nurse asked her in Spanish if she needed pain relief. She smiled and said yes. When the needle punctured her skin she began to drift off into a dream state. As the pain began to fade her confidence returned. A voice inside her told her that everything would be alright. She thanked the voice and fell gently to sleep.

Forty-eight

Ezekiel Fick had let his household staff off for the night.

He thought for sure he'd be returning with Stephanie and he had personally prepared the evening for her. Private Medical Assistance was nearby with a simple signal from his smart phone. Everything else was in the ready to take care of her—to bring her back. He could only imagine what she had been through.

But now the exchange was put off until tomorrow. He felt like a frustrated athlete who had just been told that the game was postponed. He left things as they were. He needed a night just to himself to hash over all of the events of the past two weeks. He wanted to just sit in the darkness of his library and watch the flames jump around in the fireplace.

The front part of the mansion was completely still. The only sound— an antique clock ticking from another room. Before lighting the fire Ezekiel sat by the bay window with the lights out. He could see the expanse of his property lit by a slew of decorative and functional lights that offered glow without glare.

As he stared out into the night he thought he saw the figure of a man walking along the driveway heading toward his front door. He took his

Colt Mustang and crept up by the window to get a better look. Sure enough, a man dressed in a sweatshirt and jeans was now standing on the porch. There was a gentle rap on the front door followed by a voice.

"Hey Fick, it's Arney, open up."

The old man hesitated. His cell phone went off. "Jesus Christ Zeke let me in before you blow this whole thing and end up with a corpse for a granddaughter."

Ezekiel cautiously opened the door and held his weapon at his side saying nothing. Arney bolted in as if he owned the place and headed straight for the whiskey cart in the library. Fick was edgy; he'd had enough. He pointed the barrel of the Colt at Arney and told him to put his hands up. Arney burst out laughing. "...Whoa there big fellow!" He also poured a big tumbler of whiskey for Fick.

"Put that fucking toy away and listen to me." Arney sat on the couch near the fireplace and kicked off his shoes. He gulped down his tumbler and stared at Fick waiting for an answer to a question that had not been asked.

"Here's the skinny, old man. The Feds and I think that your granddaughter was kidnapped because a certain Hollywood big shot got worked up into thinking that your uncle had left you a stash of wartime Nazi confiscated artwork which they assumed had belonged to their family." Arney paused to pour another splash. "You with me so far...?" Fick nodded.

"Okay then, When you told Chris and Chubbs that it was just the undocumented paintings of Claude Monet, dating back nearly a century which every truly snooty person in the art world thought had been destroyed around the time they were done, the Feds realized that Stephanie had been wrongly kidnapped. There is at least one showbiz type that's crapping in their pants right now because they've really stepped over the line."

The alcohol was moving quickly through Arney's bloodstream. He was about to ask Zeke for a dance. He was half out of his mind from what had happened in the past ten days since he took on this case: he'd been beaten to shit, his best friend shot and almost killed; Victor Gastaldi was murdered by person or persons unknown; and, to top things off, he'd fallen in love with Victor's hooker-mistress. Also, a witness he had interviewed committed suicide along with Victor's lesbian sister. In other words, the shit had hit the fan so often that the pungent odor was everywhere.

The tumbler of whisky had brought the elder Fick back to life. "Now see here you two-bit private dick, who in the hell do you think you are...?"

Arney shot up from the couch, snatched the Colt from Fick's hand and stuffed it into the front of the old man's slacks.

"I'll tell you who I am...I'm the guy who's gonna keep your ass out of this mess while the Feds do their job and bring the lovely Stephanie back safely. I watched you loading your SUV with firearms and supplies this afternoon." Arney thought about another shot of whisky but put it out of his mind. "You'd better leave that shit to the pros." Arney glanced around the room. "Chess...cards, porno? Whatever, but you'd better whip it out, it's going to be a long night." Arney flashed a big smile. "I'll bet you've got a hell of a refrigerator in this joint. How about a sandwich, you must be starving? I know I am!"

Forty-nine

Arney followed Fick into his kitchen. True to form, it was the size of an average hotel setup with top-of-the-line everything. Two side-by-side refrigerators grabbed Arney's attention and he had just opened the door to one of them—then it happened.

All of the electricity shut down: total darkness.

Zeke started to say something but Arney shushed him. Both men drew their weapons and stood in silence.

Arney whispered. "Unless you forgot to pay your latest utility bill my friend, I think we have company." The old man started to move but Arney told him to stand still. "Wait for a few moments until our eyes adjust." Arney was anticipating the inevitable crash of a door or a window. He didn't have to wait very long.

Somewhere in a distant room a window exploded. Arney ran over to Zeke and told him to squat down and to not move until he returned. Fick started to argue. "This is my house god damnit and I..." Arney grabbed his wrists tightly enough to cause a shot of pain. "Stay put." He dashed out of the kitchen.

Crouched down and gliding smoothly on the balls of his feet he

156

moved in the direction of the noise from the smashed window. He thought for sure that it came from the library. As he got closer he saw a pin-light moving in the darkness as if it were floating. Okay, someone is inside and looking for something. Why didn't they come looking for Zeke and Arney? Maybe they didn't think anyone was home?

Except for the light in the kitchen from this side of the mansion you wouldn't know if anyone were here. Arney kept still as he watched the intruder. He thought about shooting first and asking questions later but he had the advantage of his temporary invisibility and decided to continue to observe the stranger's movements. Within seconds the pin-light stopped moving, set on a flat surface. The thief or whatever they were was shuffling through papers at the desk hurriedly searching for something. Arney's eyes had adjusted to the darkness. The person stood with their back to him. Arney spoke. "My advice, friend, is to not move a muscle or you will definitely have a 9mil. cannon up your ass." The body froze but without a comment or physical reaction. It was as if it were not human. A soft voice floated across the room: the voice of a woman.

"Oh I don't think you'd want to have that mess on your hands, private detective Blackburn." Arney couldn't make out a face as the body turned but he was starting to have chills thinking about who it might be.

"Grandfather would be so upset if something happened to his precious little Stephanie." With that being said the ghostly face of Stephanie Fick was illuminated by the pin-light she used to find her way about in the darkness.

Arney almost fell over. "What the fuck?" He said out loud with the Colt trained on her. She lit a match and soon three candles filled the room with a surreal glow.

Stephanie leaned against the desk as if she had just finished doing her homework. Arney was about to say something when he felt a shiv in his ribcage. She smiled. "Oh by the way, do you know my friend, Danny Ballantyne?" A man's voice came from behind. "Easy there detective just let the gun fall."

Arney was too shocked to react defensively. His hand voluntarily let go and he collapsed on the floor, propped with has back against the wall.

"Well I'll be fucked. I should have known better." His head was spinning. At one time he had thought that the billionaire himself had planned his granddaughter's kidnapping but the fledgling private eye hadn't thought far enough along the trail to come up with this one.

Ezekiel Fick called out from the hallway. "Arney…what in the hell is going on?" Fick marched into the library with his weapon drawn. When he saw Stephanie he froze. "My God, baby, where did you come from? Are you okay?' He bolted towards her only to be intercepted by Danny Ballantyne who grabbed Zeke's weapon and knocked him to the floor.

It took a few seconds for the old man to realize what was going on. He looked at Arney next to him but was speechless. Arney stood up without permission. Ballantyne kept his handgun focused on the private eye.

"Well Zeke, here's one for the books." Arney looked at Stephanie. Her smile was crooked. Off-center. Just like her character.

Arney thought he now knew what had happened but he wanted to hear it from the source. He sat down on a couch and lit a cigarette. He looked over at Ballantyne. "…You mind?" Danny shrugged his shoulders. Ezekiel Fick looked like he had just gone through a series of electric shock treatments.

The private-eye exhaled slowly. He hadn't smoked a cigarette in over two years. Staring at Stephanie, he said, "Well missy, you sure fooled the entire crew. Before you and Clyde blow our brains out I sure would like to know how and why you pulled this one off?" Ballantyne addressed Stephanie as if Arney hadn't said a thing. "Did you get it?"

She smiled back at her accomplice. "Lock, stock and barrel." She giggled and Arney wanted to throw up. Ballantyne went over to grandfather Fick and bound his hands behind his back and then cold-cocked him with the barrel of his handgun. The old man groaned and fell on his side. Arney waited for her reply. She whispered something to Ballantyne and he left the room with a key ring she gave him and headed upstairs. Stephanie, now sporting her grandfather's protection sat down on the couch with Arney, the muzzle pointing toward his chest.

"Well, as all things in this world revolve around sex or money, both being vestiges of power, let's just say that my preference tends to lean toward the latter."

Arney put his cigarette out. "But Jesus Christ, you've got all of the money in the world. Why in the hell did you have to stage your own kidnapping?"

The twenty-four year old heiress to a fortune became agitated. "That's where you're wrong. *He* has all the money in the world and that son of a bitch is so fucking healthy that I'll be forty before it's mine and little good it will do me by that time!"

Arney couldn't believe his ears. What a bunch of spoiled rotten bullshit. This woman was really sick and Arney knew that he was in for it if he went sideways on her. He'd have to play the game to the max.

He surprised her with his response. "You know something I can understand where you're coming from. It's got to be a pain-in-the-ass to always be asking for what will eventually be yours." He looked up and caught a crazed look in her eyes.

He kept talking. "...But what about your parents? Where the hell are they in all of this mess?"

For the first time since being her captive Arney saw a faint glimmer of remorse in her expression. "My parents were killed in a car accident when I was twelve. Grandpa took over my upbringing after that. And I mean—took over!

"It was his fault in the first place. The overbearing bastard insisted that my father, his son, drive back from the chalet in Lake Arrowhead at midnight so that he could be at a meeting in downtown L.A. by nine. Nothing was more important to the son of a bitch than making more money. Brokering more deals, taking over more corporations. " She was feeling stressed. She began to squeeze the handle of the Colt. Arney knew that it could go off accidentally at any moment.

"I had fallen asleep earlier on the veranda when my father and grandfather came out onto the front porch arguing. The bastard accused my father of not having any balls and that if he didn't head back for that meeting right now he would cut him off without a dime.

My mother was crying when she found me on the porch and took me inside to put me to bed. My father wanted her to stay with me but she insisted on going with him to share the driving. They could be back the following night." Stephanie loosened her grip on the handgun looking down at the floor. "He didn't even say goodbye to me. He grabbed my mother and they tore out of the driveway in their Caddy. On the return trip, about half way back, their car crossed the dividing line on the interstate and they went head-first into a sixteen-wheeler. The best guess from the Highway Patrol was that whoever was driving fell asleep at the wheel."

Arney needed to buy more time. "But why in the hell would you have yourself kidnapped?"

Stephanie Fick smiled with pleasure recalling her plan and its fool-proof potential. "Two years ago I was going through the attic looking for some photos of mom and dad that the bastard had put in storage. He didn't even have one picture of my parents in the mansion. I stumbled onto a small unmarked file cabinet. Inside were letters translated from German into English regarding my great grand-parents and an uncle of my grandfather's named Roderich. There were details about some partially destroyed Monet canvasses which were left to grandfather after the war. I did some research and discovered the trail of mystery which surrounded all of the looted art work which the Hitler regime had confiscated during the Second World War. Soon after that it struck me. I began to fantasize about a way to get his fortune without waiting around for the bastard to die. My plan was a simple one based on guilt. I found out that grandfather's uncle was a Nazi architect. Ole' Zeke wouldn't want anyone to know about that connection." Stephanie let out a sardonic laugh that gave Arney a chill. The P.I. was staring into her face with that look a prime-time journalist has when doing an interview on camera: serious concern mixed with anticipation. He needed to keep her talking while he tried to figure a way out of this mess.

Stephanie lit a cigarette and exhaled heavily. "I hadn't seen my brother in a few years. He moved to the Chicago Stock Exchange and I flew out to spend some time with him.

"I met Ballantyne while soaking up the atmosphere in a bar on the south side. We hung out for a couple of days and I asked him to go with me to the Sundance Film Festival. He was the first rough and tumble man I had been around. Great sex. I think I was in love with the guy from the first moment I met him." Arney wasn't sure where this was going but so far he was still breathing. He gave her a smile of encouragement to continue.

"One night at the Pioneer bar, my new playmate ran into an old high-school buddy from Chicago. He happened to be one of the most famous directors in Hollywood. His name is Howard Solomon, you know of him?"

Arney shrugged his shoulders. "I don't go to the movies very much."

"Figures." Stephanie used her free hand to light another cigarette while scanning the library door waiting for Danny to return from upstairs.

"Through my research I'd discovered that there was a segment of Hollywood stars who had organized to have these stolen art treasures returned. Suddenly the whole thing clicked. I took Danny aside and told him about the plan I had been hatching for months. He was all for it. By the end of the evening we had everything in place with a famous fall guy lined up to take the heat when it came down.

"I paid Danny to hire a crew and we plotted the kidnapping down to the last degree. Every step of the way looked real. I spent the whole time in the stash-house in Long Beach only getting out of bed around midnight to stretch my legs for an hour then back to bed. They kept me high on morphine. Great dreams."

Stephanie was becoming impatient. "We put that video together and sent it to grandfather. The letters I found in the attic gave me all the info I needed. Danny called about the exchange and we came tonight to get the necessary papers to cash in. Then, the two of us disappear and no one knows what happened to Stephanie Fick. When Danny finishes upstairs we're out of here."

She gave Arney an evil smile. "Of course you and Zeke will have to stay behind…permanently!"

Ezekiel was beginning to stir. Stephanie walked over to him and slammed his head with the grip of the pistol and he headed back to the floor, groaning. With her weapon trained on Arney she moved to the door of the library and yelled out. "Danny…what the fuck are you doing up there? Let's go!"

At that moment there was a huge noise which sounded like a dozen bowling balls set in motion. Stephanie jumped out into the hallway just in time to see Ballantyne careening down the stairs rolling like a tumbler in a circus act.

She moved quickly toward his crumpled body, her weapon trained on the second floor landing. Arney was about to jump into action when he saw someone move out of the darkness of the hallway with their weapon drawn. The shadowy figure pressed the barrel into her back. It was Chris Clarke.

"That will be enough Ms. Fick. Lower your weapon slowly." She hesitated but Chris didn't. He grabbed her gun arm so fiercely that something snapped. She let out one hell of a scream and he pushed her onto the floor kneeling on her back, cuffing her hands behind her. Meanwhile Chubbs came down the stairs casually whistling as he descended. He stepped over the bruised and battered body of Danny Ballantyne, bent down and cuffed him, then joined Chris and Stephanie.

Chris looked over at Arney. "You okay Blackburn?"

"Just like the fucking Cavalry. Yeah, I'm okay but we'd better check grandpa, he took a hell of a whack from his precious granddaughter." Chubbs hurried over to Zeke and moved the old man onto the couch.

Within minutes the area came to life with ambulances, fire trucks, police cars, FBI vehicles and forensic teams. The front of the property looked like a jammed parking lot for a sporting event. The collective illumination supplied by all the different county departments gave the atmosphere a day-time glow.

Dozens of officials from the Mayor's office on up or down were gathered at three in the morning assessing the damage. Uniformed officers as well as forensic personnel took over the crime scene. Arney headed toward the kitchen with Chris and Chubbs in tow.

It was all over, but there were still a lot of loose ends to tie up.

CHAPTER FIFTY

Arney finally made himself a sandwich. Chris and Chubbs were around the kitchen table drinking coffee provided by the fire department. Blackburn took a nervous bite, glancing from Chris to Chubbs with his mouth full and barely audible. "So, how in the fuck did you guys end up here? What the hell happened?"

Chris leaned in. "I went to L.A. General to interview Conchita. You see, although we have no proof, it has been my contention that she killed Gastaldi. In her weakened state I thought she might confess but she wasn't buying it.

"The longer I stared at her while she was denying my allegations, the more I realized how unique a woman she really is. She is truly an incredible female: street smart, intuitive, naturally intelligent, drop-dead gorgeous and of course, a great manipulator. That last attribute is a big one in her favor." Chris paused to light another cigarette glancing with a smile at his two partners. "She certainly didn't have to work that hard to wrap you both around her little finger." Arney and Chubbs shifted uneasily in their chairs.

"Hey, don't get me wrong. It's not hard to see why she was so capable of sucking you both in. But that made me start to think about our kidnapping. What if we were dealing with another incredibly strong woman who had an agenda and was ready, willing and able to pull it off?"

Arney gulped down a bite and said; "...But why should that thought even occur to you? Jesus Christ, I never would have dreamed that the victim was the perpetrator on this one."

Chris looked around the kitchen willing another cup of coffee to float over to him. "Well to be honest, I had a little help. A panicked phone call came into the Washington Bureau from an American citizen in the Mid-East. As it turns out, this caller was on Abe's list; one of the most prestigious film directors around today.

"He's shooting a movie in Tunisia. When he saw the news of the kidnapping on the Net, he confessed over the phone to knowing about the plan as he was an ex-high-school-buddy of Ballantyne's and they had actually been with him when he and his female companion hatched the idea. Mr. Academy-Award- winner said that they were pitching it to him as a possible plot for a screenplay." Chris paused with a big smile. "My bet is the son of a bitch was in on it to some degree, that's how they got the cinema-ready video clip that we saw on Fick's computer. The description of the female with Ballantyne coughed up by Solomon was a dead ringer for our victim. I got my usual chills when I heard that."

Chubbs started to laugh. "Oh yeah my man does get chills when he is near the finishing line."

An extremely exhausted Chief McCreary wandered into the kitchen, bringing with him a thermos of coffee. He sat down heavily and placed the thermos in the middle of the table. He cast an exasperated look at Arney. "Well son, you've done it again. Why in the hell didn't you keep me posted as the events were progressing? All of the sudden this case blows wide open and I've got some messenger from the mayor's office telling me all about it. That put me damn near last in line..."

Arney cut in. "Whoa Mac, don't have a heart attack. If it will make you feel any better I didn't know what the hell was going on until it hit me smack in the face." Arney grabbed the thermos just as Chris was about to reach for it. "Look, who-da thunk that the bitch was the bad guy!" He smiled at Chris and poured him a cup. "I just came out here to keep grandpa Fick out of the thick of it. I had no idea that the case would come to a bang and a boom tonight. Give me a break Mac."

Chris jumped in. "Honestly Chief, you were dead on about the possible participation of some of Hollywood's finest." Chris addressed Mac as he sipped his coffee. "Actually, I think that Mr. Academy Awards had more to do with it than he claims but that would be hard to prove unless we get collaboration from our two suspects."

The four men seated at the kitchen table jumped to their feet at the same time as several rounds of rapid gunfire went off within a few seconds. Weapons drawn, the quartet headed for the front of the house where all hell had broken loose. There, standing in the hallway with his Colt Mustang dangling from his right hand was Ezekiel Fick. Lying on the ground at his feet was the motionless body of Danny Ballantyne.

Fick saw the lawmen approaching him and threw his hand gun gently in their direction. "I don't care what happens to me, but this scumbag had to go." The old man sat at the foot of the stairs with his head in his hands and began to cry.

A few seconds later police officers handcuffed Fick and took him away. Stephanie had already been taken downtown. Chief Mac, Arney, Chris and Chubbs just stood there with no reaction. Finally Arney broke the silence.

"Now what…?"

No one had been watching Ezekiel Fick after he was attended to by the county paramedics. When he realized that, he walked over to where his Colt had been marked as evidence on the floor, picked it up and walked out of the library just as officers were taking Ballantyne away.

He shot him six times. He would probably be prosecuted but not convicted. Anyone who could speed-dial the President of the United States could probably acquire a "get out of jail free" card.

Epilogue

Baja Mexico was showing off its sunshine for the patrons of the Rosarita Beach Hotel. The sparsely developed coast-line just south of San Diego near Ensenada was caught in a time capsule.

With all of the real estate property development on the sandy shores from Baja to northern California, this stretch of beach didn't seem to be aware or for that matter, care. The hotel with its Spanish-influenced architecture was nearly a century old and famed for its design.

In the nineteen-thirties it catered to the Hollywood crowd; stars like Clark Gable and Carole Lombard used the calm atmosphere of the Mexican Riviera to escape the pressures of their public lives.

Due to the exclusivity of the hotel's location and the massive number of millionaires born into society the hotel took on a five star rating and prices to match. Whoever has recently enjoyed a stay at this legendary oasis has come away impressed with the quality of service and the sheer opulence that travels along the wind-blown corridors as the privilege of just being there causes a relaxation that few venues can offer.

Everyone from the most common tourist to European Royalty has scuffed the magnificently colored tiled floors of the lobby over the decades. The white-washed adobe walls, thick enough to resist cannon fire, topped off with red-clay tile roofs that extend forever, offer a piece of paradise for those who have enough money to never think about what it's costing.

The maid was trying to get away to smoke a cigarette but her employer kept calling for something every five minutes. First her Chanel Sunglasses, all six pairs so she could decide which to wear when she went down to the swimming pool.

Then it was the never-ending errands to fetch and display the woman's wardrobe which could have clothed half the female population of Ensenada.

And as if that wasn't enough, her new Matron wasn't even thirty years old and having recently turned forty-five, the maid was having a few problems being bossed around by someone so young.

When she brought the half-dozen pair of sunglasses into the bedroom of the hotel suite, the woman was on the phone ordering room service. She paused and asked the servant if she would like anything?

What the hell was this all about? She shyly requested a sandwich and a coke. The woman placed the order then hung up the phone offering the maid a warm smile.

"You know, Serena, I really like you. You're very good at what you do. I have absolutely no complaints. I want you to think about leaving here with me in a permanent position." The young woman winked at her as she stood allowing her robe to fall to the floor. She was completely naked.

Serena tried not to respond but it was difficult. The woman had a great body and she was moving over toward the bed, still smiling. She pulled herself onto the satin cover then held her arms out inviting the maid to join her. Serena wasn't sure what to do. She approached the bed hesitantly and stopped about a foot away. The woman turned her back toward her. "Would you be so kind as to massage my shoulders? I'm so tense."

The maid pulled a chair up to the edge of the bed and placed her hands on the woman's shoulders. She began to massage very lightly and slowly.

The woman sighed after the first touch. "Oh, I just knew that you would have great hands." Serena dug in a little harder and the woman began to breathe heavily.

Just then a knock at the door: room service.

The woman pulled herself off of the bed and threw on her robe. "Tell them to set it up on the balcony. We'll have a bite together. Okay?"

Two hours later Serena crawled out of bed after a sexual encounter she had never imagined was possible. She had never been with another woman but this young beauty had satisfied her more than any man had in her life.

She was floating upon the ecstasy of the moment when reality peeked over her shoulder. She went into the bathroom to prepare madam's bath. While the water was running she looked at her own naked body in the floor to ceiling mirror. She was awakening to the fact that she was still desirable, even in middle-age. She was in fact, beautiful.

Conchita Morales rolled over to look at herself in the mirror. It was so dark that she really couldn't see. It was just a habit she had picked up along the road. She was now set for life.

When she was released from the hospital she dug up the files on the hard-drive disks of Victor's dealings with the local politicians and police. When she contacted the parties involved they had no problem paying her off to get lost. As a little insurance, she made copies of the accounts and sent them to her high-powered attorney in Beverly Hills. She informed those involved that if anything happened to her...well, you know.

She called to Serena to bring her a bottle of sparkling water. She planned on living like this until the end. Yes, she'd been a cheap prostitute, a first class call-girl and just a plain whore. But she could now just catalogue that period of her life as experience and nothing more.

Serena came into the bedroom with a tray and set it down on the bed. Conchita took a Franklin out of her purse and handed it to her. "Go out tonight and have a blast. But be back here by midnight. Wake me if I'm asleep. Understand?"

Serena nodded and left the room.

The maid gathered up her things and went down to the lobby bar. She ordered bourbon on the rocks and sat in a daze staring at the bartender. He came back over. "You need something else lady?

"Maybe—maybe not." She downed the cocktail in one gulp and headed out the door realizing that life was about to change— drastically.

Dear reader,

I hope you've enjoyed *Deadly Impressions*. An author's capacity to remain visible in the crowded forum of countless other writers is the all-so-important reader review. It's a simple process and only requires a few minutes of your time. Merely go to my Amazon site and the instructions are clearly presented. It's up to you: a few words or an entire critique. Your efforts do not go unnoticed by myself, as an author, or by persons who rely on reading reviews to influence their next purchase. Compliments as well as critical remarks are equally valued. A review becomes a vital clue to an author as to what aspects of their design are working on the imagination of the reader. I read each review and take the remarks to heart. So if you have the time, let me know what you think of my efforts. It means a lot to me.

Thanks,
Art Johnson

Acknowledgments

Special thanks to Irish poet John Montague and author Elizabeth Wassel for their encouragement and faith from the beginning. To author F.J Dagg for his constant questioning of my motives throughout this work.

To my wife, Patricia who never doubts. To Ronnie Pontiac and Tamra who got the ball rolling years ago. To Chi-Li Wong whose support has been constant, and finally to Kenneth Atchity who has been my guide through the dark forest of story-telling.

About the Author

Art Johnson was born in San Diego, California in 1945. He contracted Polio Paralysis in 1950. Undaunted by the physical restriction, he became a musician, and moved to Hollywood in 1968. As a studio and touring professional he has recorded and performed with artists such as Lena Horne, Barbra Streisand and Luciano Pavarotti. He is a Grammy and Academy Award winning participant for music. As a solo recording artist with eight CDs to his credit, he is the executive consultant for a prominent jazz record label in the U.S.

He began writing in the 1980's while working at The Philosophical Research Society in Los Angeles as one of several assistant to Manly Palmer Hall. He lectured at the Society for four years, on the subjects of Humanities and the Arts focusing on poetry and poets.

In 1990 Art returned to San Diego to become an adjunct faculty member of the San Diego Symphony. He holds an MA for music and was formerly a professor of improvisational studies at San Diego State University before moving to France in 2003. He currently resides in Monaco with his wife Patricia, where he continues to record and write.

www.ingramcontent.com/pod-product-compliance
Lightning Source LLC
Chambersburg PA
CBHW050738250626
47155CB00005B/1826

* 9 7 8 0 9 9 6 3 6 8 9 0 2 *